Gabbi tilted her chin

"Suitable marriages," she began fearlessly, "are manipulated among the wealthy for numerous reasons. Love isn't a necessary requisite."

Benedict's expression didn't change, but she sensed a degree of anger. "And what we share in bed? How would you define that?"

A lump rose in her throat. "Skilled expertise."

"You'd relegate me to a position of *stud?*"

"*No.* No," she reiterated, stricken. She closed her eyes. He was angry. And it hurt, terribly. Yet what had she expected? A declaration that she was too important in his life for him to consider anyone taking her place?

HELEN BIANCHIN was born in New Zealand and traveled to Australia before marrying her Italian-born husband. After three years they moved, returned to New Zealand with their daughter, had two sons, then resettled in Australia. Encouraged by friends to recount anecdotes of her years as a tobacco sharefarmer's wife living in an Italian community, Helen began setting words on paper and her first novel was published in 1975. An animal lover, she says her terrier and Persian cat regard her study as as much theirs as hers!

Books by Helen Bianchin

HELEN BIANCHIN

An Ideal Marriage?

Harlequin Books

TORONTO • NEW YORK • LONDON
AMSTERDAM • PARIS • SYDNEY • HAMBURG
STOCKHOLM • ATHENS • TOKYO • MILAN
MADRID • WARSAW • BUDAPEST • AUCKLAND

ISBN 0-373-11905-4

AN IDEAL MARRIAGE?

First North American Publication 1997.

CHAPTER ONE

GABBI eased the car to a halt in the long line of traffic banked up behind the New South Head Road intersection adjacent to Sydney's suburban Elizabeth Bay. A slight frown creased her forehead as she checked her watch, and her fingers tapped an impatient tattoo against the steering wheel.

She had precisely one hour in which to shower, wash her hair, dry and style it, apply make-up, dress, and greet invited dinner guests. The loss of ten minutes caught up in heavy traffic didn't form part of her plan.

Her eyes slid to the manicured length of her nails, and she dwelt momentarily on the fact that time spent on their lacquered perfection had cost her her lunch. An apple at her desk mid-afternoon could hardly be termed an adequate substitute.

The car in front began to move, and she followed its path, picking up speed, only to depress the brake pedal as the lights changed.

Damn. At this rate it would take two, if not three attempts to clear the intersection.

She *should*, she admitted silently, have left her office earlier in order to miss the heavy early evening traffic. Yet stubborn single-mindedness had prevented her from doing so.

As James Stanton's daughter, she had no need to

work. Property, an extensive share portfolio and a handsome annuity placed her high on the list of Sydney's independently wealthy young women.

As Benedict Nicols' *wife*, her position as assistant management consultant with Stanton-Nicols Enterprises was viewed as nepotism at its very worst.

Gabbi thrust the gear-shift forward with unaccustomed force, attaining momentary satisfaction from the sound of the Mercedes' refined engine as she eased the car forward and followed the traffic's crawling pace, only to halt scant minutes later.

The cellphone rang, and she automatically reached for it.

'Gabrielle.'

Only one person steadfastly refused to abbreviate her Christian name. 'Monique.'

'You're driving?'

'Stationary,' she informed her, pondering the purpose of her stepmother's call. Monique never rang to simply say 'hello.'

'Annaliese flew in this afternoon. Would it be an imposition if she came to dinner?'

Years spent attending an élite boarding-school had instilled requisite good manners. 'Not at all. We'd be delighted.'

'Thank you, darling.'

Monique's voice sounded like liquid satin as she ended the call.

Wonderful, Gabbi accorded silently as she punched in the appropriate code and alerted Marie to set another place at the table.

'Sorry to land this on you,' she added apologetically before replacing the handset down onto the console. An extra guest posed no problem, and Gabbi wasn't sufficiently superstitious to consider thirteen at the table a premise for an unsuccessful evening.

The traffic began to move, and the faint tension behind her eyes threatened to develop into a headache.

James Stanton's remarriage ten years ago to a twenty-nine-year-old divorcee with one young daughter had gifted him with a contentment Gabbi could never begrudge him. Monique was his social equal, and an exemplary hostess. It was unfortunate that Monique's affection didn't extend to James's daughter. As a vulnerable fifteen-year-old Gabbi had sensed her stepmother's superficiality, and spent six months agonising over why, until a friend had spelled out the basic psychology of a dysfunctional relationship.

In retaliation, Gabbi had chosen to excel at everything she did—she'd striven to gain straight As in each subject, had won sporting championships, and graduated from university with an honours degree in business management. She'd studied languages and spent a year in Paris, followed by another in Tokyo, before returning to Sydney to work for a rival firm. Then she'd applied for and won, on the strength of her experience and credentials, a position with Stanton-Nicols.

There was a certain danger in allowing one's thoughts to dwell on the past, Gabbi mused a trifle wryly as she swung the Mercedes into the exclusive Vaucluse street, where heavy, wide-branched trees added a certain ambience to the luxurious homes nestled out of sight behind high concrete walls.

A few hundred metres along she drew the car to a halt, depressed a remote modem, and waited the necessary seconds as the double set of ornate black wrought-iron gates slid smoothly aside.

A wide curved driveway led to an elegant two-storeyed Mediterranean-style home set well back from the road in beautiful landscaped grounds. Encompassing four allotments originally acquired in the late 1970s by Conrad Nicols, the existing four houses had been removed to make way for a multi-million-dollar residence whose magnificent harbour views placed it high in Sydney's real-estate stratosphere.

Ten years later extensive million-dollar refurbishment had added extensions providing additional bedroom accommodation, garages for seven cars, remodelled kitchen, undercover terraces, and balconies. The revamped gardens boasted fountains, courtyards, ornamental ponds and English-inspired lawns bordered by clipped hedges.

It was incredibly sad, Gabbi reflected as she released one set of automatic garage doors and drove beneath them, that Conrad and Diandra Nicols had been victims of a freak highway accident mere weeks after the final landscaping touches had been completed.

Yet Conrad had achieved in death what he hadn't achieved in the last ten years of his life: His son and heir had returned from America and taken over Conrad's partnership in Stanton-Nicols.

Gabbi slid the Mercedes to a halt between the sleek lines of Benedict's XJ220 Jaguar and the more staid frame of a black Bentley. Missing was the top-of-therange four-wheel drive Benedict used to commute each day to the city.

The garage doors slid down with a refined click and Gabbi caught up her briefcase from the passenger seat, slipped out from behind the wheel, then crossed to a side door to punch in a series of digits, deactivating the security system guarding entry to the house.

Mansion, she corrected herself with a twisted smile as she lifted the in-house phone and rang through to the kitchen. 'Hi, Marie. Everything under control?'

Twenty years' service with the Nicols family enabled the housekeeper to respond with a warm chuckle. 'No problems.'

'Thanks,' Gabbi acknowledged gratefully before hurrying through the wide hallway to a curved staircase leading to the upper floor.

Marie would be putting the final touches to the four-course meal she'd prepared; her husband, Serg, would be checking the temperature of the wines Benedict had chosen to be served, and Sophie, the casual help, would be running a final check of the dining-room.

All *she* had to do was appear downstairs, perfectly groomed, when Serg answered the ring of the doorbell and ushered the first of their guests into the lounge in around forty minutes.

Or less, Gabbi accorded as she ascended the stairs at a rapid pace.

Benedict's mother had chosen lush-piled eau-de-nil carpet and pale textured walls to offset the classic lines of the mahogany furniture, employing a skilful blend of toning colour with matching drapes and bed-covers, ensuring each room was subtly different.

The master suite was situated in the eastern wing with glass doors opening onto two balconies and commanding impressive views of the harbour. Panoramic by day, those views became a magical vista at night, with a fairy-like tracery of distant electric and flashing neon light.

Gabbi kicked off her shoes, removed jewellery, then quickly shed her clothes *en route* to a marble-tiled *en suite* which almost rivalled the bedroom in size.

Elegantly decadent in pale gold-streaked ivory marble, there was a huge spa-bath and a double shower to complement the usual facilities.

Ten minutes later she entered the bedroom, a towel fastened sarong-style over her slim curves, with another wound into a turban on top of her head.

'Cutting it fine, Gabbi?' Benedict's faintly accented drawl held a mocking edge as he shrugged off his suit jacket and loosened his tie.

In his late thirties, tall, with a broad, hard-muscled frame, his sculpted facial features gave a hint of his maternal Andalusian ancestry. Dark, almost black eyes held a powerful intensity that never softened for his fellow man, and rarely for a woman.

'Whatever happened to "Hi, honey, I'm home"?' she retaliated as she crossed the room and selected fresh underwear from a recessed drawer, hurriedly donned briefs and bra, then stepped into a silk slip.

'Followed by a salutatory kiss?' he mocked with a

tinge of musing cynicism as he shed his shirt and attended to the zip of his trousers.

She felt the tempo of her heartbeat increase, and she was conscious of an elevated tension that began in the pit of her stomach and flared along every nerve-end, firing her body with an acute awareness that was entirely physical.

Dynamic masculinity at its most potent, she acknowledged silently as she snatched up a silk robe, thrust her arms through its sleeves, and retraced her steps to the *en suite*.

Removing the towelled turban, she caught up the hair-drier and began blow-drying her hair.

Her attention rapidly became unfocused as Benedict entered the *en suite* and crossed to the shower. Mirrored walls reflected his naked image, and she determinedly ignored the olive-toned skin sheathing hard muscle and sinew, the springy dark hair that covered his chest and arrowed down past his waist to reach his manhood, the firmly shaped buttocks, and the powerful length of his back.

Her eyes followed the powerful strength of his shoulders as he reached forward to activate the flow of water, then the glass doors slid closed behind him.

Gabbi tugged the brush through her hair with unnecessary force, and felt her eyes prick at the sudden pain.

It was one year, two months and three weeks since their marriage, and she still couldn't handle the effect he had on her in bed or out of it.

Her scalp tingled in protest, and she relaxed the brushstrokes then switched off the drier. Her hair was still slightly damp, its natural ash-blonde colour appearing faintly darker, highlighting the creamy smoothness of her skin and accentuating the deep blue of her eyes.

With practised movements she caught the length of her hair and deftly swept it into a chignon at her nape, secured it with pins, then began applying make-up.

Minutes later she heard the water stop, and with conscious effort she focused on blending her eyeshadow, studiously ignoring him as he crossed to the long marbled pedestal and began dealing with a day's growth of beard.

'Bad day?'

Her fingers momentarily stilled, then she replaced the eyeshadow palette and selected mascara. 'Why do you ask?'

'You have expressive eyes,' Benedict observed as he smoothed his fingers over his jaw.

Gabbi met his gaze in the mirror, and held it. 'Annaliese is to be a last-minute guest at dinner.'

He switched off the electric shaver and reached for the cut-glass bottle containing an exclusive brand of cologne. 'That bothers you?'

She tried for levity. 'I'm capable of slaying my own dragons.'

One eyebrow lifted with sardonic humour. 'Verbal swords over dessert?'

Annaliese was known not to miss an opportunity, and Gabbi couldn't imagine tonight would prove an exception. 'I'll do my best to parry any barbs with practised civility.'

His eyes swept over her slim curves then returned

to study the faint, brooding quality evident on her finely etched features, and a slight smile tugged the edges of his mouth. 'The objective being to win another battle in an ongoing war?'

'Has anyone beaten *you* in battle, Benedict?' she queried lightly as she capped the mascara wand, returned it to the drawer housing her cosmetics and concentrated on applying a soft pink colour to her lips.

He didn't answer. He had no need to assert that he was a man equally feared and respected by his contemporaries and rarely, if ever, fooled by anyone.

Just watch my back. The words remained unuttered as she turned towards the door, and minutes later she selected a long black pencil-slim silk skirt and teamed it with a simple scoop-necked sleeveless black top. Stiletto-heeled evening shoes completed the outfit, and she added a pear-shaped diamond pendant and matching ear-studs, then slipped on a slim, diamond-encrusted bracelet before turning towards the mirror to cast her reflection a cursory glance. A few dabs of her favourite Le Must de Cartier perfume added the final touch.

'Ready?'

Gabbi turned at the sound of his voice, and felt her breath catch at the image he presented.

There was something about his stance, a sense of animalistic strength, that fine tailoring did little to tame. The dramatic mesh of elemental ruthlessness and primitive power added a magnetism few women of any age could successfully ignore.

For a few timeless seconds her eyes locked with his

in an attempt to determine what lay behind the studied inscrutability he always managed to portray.

She envied him his superb control…and wondered what it would take to break it.

'Yes.' Her voice was steady, and she summoned a bright smile as she turned to precede him from the room.

The main staircase curved down to the ground floor in an elegant sweep of wide, partially carpeted marble stairs, with highly polished mahogany bannisters supported by ornately scrolled black wrought-iron balusters.

Set against floor-to-ceiling lead-panelled glass, the staircase created an elegant focus highlighted by a magnificent crystal chandelier.

Marble floors lent spaciousness and light to the large entry foyer, sustained by textured ivory-coloured walls whose uniformity was broken by a series of wide, heavily panelled doors, works of art, and a collection of elegant Mediterranean-style cabinets.

Gabbi had just placed a foot on the last stair when the doorbell pealed.

'Show-time,' she murmured as Serg emerged from the eastern hallway and moved quickly towards the impressively panelled double front doors.

Benedict's eyes hardened fractionally. 'Cynicism doesn't suit you.'

Innate pride lent her eyes a fiery sparkle, and her chin tilted slightly in a gesture of mild defiance. 'I can be guaranteed to behave,' she assured him quietly, and felt her pulse quicken as he caught hold of her hand.

'Indeed.' The acknowledgement held a dry softness which was lethal, and an icy chill feathered across the surface of her skin.

'Charles,' Benedict greeted smoothly seconds later as Serg announced the first of their guests. 'Andrea.' His smile was warm, and he appeared relaxed and totally at ease. 'Come through to the lounge and let me get you a drink.'

Most of the remaining guests arrived within minutes, and Gabbi played her role as hostess to the hilt, circulating, smiling, all the time waiting for the moment Monique and Annaliese would precede her father into the lounge.

Monique believed in making an entrance, and her arrival was always carefully timed to provide maximum impact. While she was never unpardonably late, her timing nevertheless bordered on the edge of social acceptability.

Serg's announcement coincided with Gabbi's expectation and, excusing herself from conversation, she moved forward to greet her father.

'James.' She brushed his cheek with her lips and accepted the firm clasp on her shoulder in return before turning towards her stepmother to accept the salutatory air-kiss. 'Monique.' Her smile was without fault as she acknowledged the stunning young woman at Monique's side. 'Annaliese. How nice to see you.'

Benedict joined her, the light touch of his hand at the back of her waist a disturbing sensation that provided subtle reassurance and a hidden warning. That it also succeeded in sharpening her senses and made her incredibly aware of him was entirely a secondary consideration.

His greeting echoed her own, his voice assuming a subtle inflection that held genuine warmth with her father, utter charm with her stepmother, and an easy tolerance with Annaliese.

Monique's sweet smile in response was faultless. Annaliese, however, was pure feline and adept in the art of flirtation. A skill she seemed to delight in practising on any male past the age of twenty, with scant respect for his marital status.

'Benedict.' With just one word Annaliese managed to convey a wealth of meaning that set Gabbi's teeth on edge.

The pressure of Benedict's fingers increased, and Gabbi gave him a stunning smile, totally ignoring the warning flare in the depths of those dark eyes.

Dinner was a success. It would have been difficult for even the most discerning gourmand's palate to find fault with the serving of fine food beautifully cooked, superbly presented, and complemented by excellent wine.

Benedict was an exemplary host, and his inherent ability to absorb facts and figures combined with an almost photographic memory ensured conversation was varied and interesting. Men sought and valued his opinion on a business level, and envied him his appeal with women. Women, on the other hand, sought his attention and coveted Gabbi's position as his wife.

A MATCH MADE IN HEAVEN, the tabloids had announced at the time. THE WEDDING OF THE DECADE, a number of women's magazines had headlined, depicting a variety of photographs to endorse the projected image.

Only the romantically inclined accepted the media coverage as portrayed, while the city's—indeed, the entire country's—upper social echelons recognised the facts beneath the fairy floss.

The marriage of Benedict Nicols and Gabrielle Stanton had occurred as a direct result of the manipulative strategy by James Stanton to cement the Stanton-Nicols financial empire and forge it into another generation.

The reason for Benedict's participation was clear...he stood to gain total control of Stanton-Nicols. The bonus was a personable young woman eminently eligible to sire the necessary progeny.

Gabbi's compliance had been motivated in part by a desire to please her father and the realistic recognition that, given his enormous wealth, there would be very few men, if any, who would discount the financial and social advantage of being James Stanton's son-in-law.

'Shall we adjourn to the lounge for coffee?'

The smooth words caught Gabbi's attention, and she took Benedict's cue by summoning a gracious smile and rising to her feet. 'I'm sure Marie has it ready.'

'Treasure of a chef', 'wonderful meal', 'delightful evening'. Words echoed in polite praise, and she inclined her head in acknowledgement. 'Thank you. I'll pass on your compliments to Marie. She'll be pleased.' Which was true. Marie valued the high salary and separate live-in accommodation that formed part of the employment package, and her gratitude was reflected in her culinary efforts.

'You were rather quiet at dinner, darling.'

Gabbi heard Monique's softly toned voice, and turned towards her. 'Do you think so?'

'Annaliese is a little hurt, I think.' The reproach was accompanied by a wistful smile, and Gabbi allowed her eyes to widen slightly.

'Oh, dear,' she managed with credible regret. 'She gave such a convincing display of enjoying herself.'

Monique's eyes assumed a mistiness Gabbi knew to be contrived. *How did she do that?* Her stepmother had missed her vocation; as an actress she would have excelled.

'Annaliese has always regarded you as an elder sister.'

There was nothing *familial* about Annaliese's regard—for Gabbi. Benedict, however, fell into an entirely different category.

'I'm deeply flattered,' Gabbi acknowledged gently, and incurred Monique's sharp glance. They had lingered slightly behind the guests exiting the dining-room and were temporarily out of their earshot.

'She's very fond of you.'

Doubtful. Gabbi had always been regarded as a rival, and Annaliese was her mother's daughter. Perfectly groomed, beautifully dressed, perfumed…and on a mission. To tease and tantalise, and enjoy the challenge of the chase until she caught the right man.

Gabbi was saved from making a response as they entered the lounge, and she accepted coffee from Marie, choosing to take it black, strong and sweet.

With a calm that was contrived she lifted her cup and took a sip of the strong, aromatic brew. 'If you'll excuse me? I really must have a word with James.'

It was almost midnight when the last guest departed, a time deemed neither too early nor too late for a mid-week dinner party to end.

Gabbi slid off her heeled sandals as she crossed the foyer to the lounge. Her head felt impossibly heavy, a knot of tension twisting a painful path from her right temple down to the edge of her nape.

Sophie had cleared the remaining coffee cups and liqueur glasses, and in the morning Marie would ensure the lounge was restored to its usual immaculate state.

'A successful evening, wouldn't you agree?'

Benedict's lazy drawl stirred the embers of resentment she'd kept carefully banked over the past few hours.

'How could it not be?' she countered as she turned to face him.

'You want to orchestrate a post-mortem?' he queried with deceptive mildness, and she glimpsed the tightly coiled strength beneath the indolent façade.

'Not particularly.'

He conducted a brief, encompassing appraisal of her features. 'Then I suggest you go upstairs to bed.'

Her chin tilted fractionally, and she met his dark gaze with equanimity. 'And prepare myself to accommodate you?'

There was a flicker of something dangerous in the depths of his eyes, then it was gone, and his movements as he closed the distance between them held a smooth, panther-like grace.

'*Accommodate?*' he stressed silkily.

He was too close, his height and broad frame an intimidating entity that invaded her space. The clean, male smell of him combined with his exclusive brand of cologne weakened her defences and lodged an attack against the very core of her femininity.

He had no need to touch her, and it irked her unbearably that he knew it.

'Your sexual appetite is...' Gabbi paused, then added delicately, 'Consistent.' Her eyes flared slightly, the blue depths pure crystalline sapphire.

He lifted a hand and caught hold of her chin, lifting it so she had little option but to retain his gaze. 'It's a woman's prerogative to decline.'

She looked at him carefully, noting the fine lines fanning out from the corners of his eyes, the deep vertical crease slashing each cheek, and the firm, sensual lines of his mouth.

The tug of sexual awareness intensified at the thought of the havoc that mouth could wreak when it possessed her own, the pleasure as it explored the soft curves of her body.

'And a man's inclination to employ unfair persuasion,' Gabbi offered, damning the slight catch of her breath as the pad of his thumb traced an evocative pattern along the edge of her jaw, then slid down the pulsing cord to the hollow at the curve of her neck, cupping it while he loosened the pins holding her hair in place.

They fell to the carpet as his fingers combed the

blonde length free, then his head lowered and she closed her eyes as his lips brushed her temple, then feathered a path to the edge of her mouth, teasing its outline as he tested the soft fullness and sensed the faint trembling as she tried for control.

She should stop him now, plead tiredness, the existence of a headache...say she didn't want to have to try to cope with the aftermath of his lovemaking. The futility of experiencing utter joy and knowing physical lust was an unsatisfactory substitute for love.

His body moved in close against her own, its hard length a potent force she fought hard to ignore. Without success, for she had little defence against the firm pressure of his lips as he angled her mouth and possessed it, gently at first, then with an increasing depth of passion which demanded her capitulation.

She didn't care when she felt his hands slide the length of her skirt up over her thighs, and she cared even less when he shaped her buttocks and lifted her up against him.

There was a sense of exultant pleasure as she curved her legs around his hips and tangled her arms together behind his neck, the movement of his body an exciting enticement as he ascended the stairs to their bedroom.

She was on fire, *aching* for the feel of his skin against her own, and her fingers feverishly freed his tie and attacked the buttons on his shirt, not satisfied until they found the silken whorls of hair covering his taut, muscled chest.

Her mouth slid down the firm column of his throat,

savoured the hollow at its base, then sought a tantalising path along one collarbone.

At some stage she became dimly aware she was standing, her clothes, and *his* no longer a barrier, and she gave a soft cry as he pulled her down onto the bed.

Now, hard and fast. No preliminaries. And afterwards he could take all the time he wanted.

His deep, husky laugh brought faint colour to her cheeks. A colour that deepened at the comprehension that she'd inadvertently said the words out loud.

He sank into her, watching her expressive features as she accepted him, the fleeting changes as she stretched and the slight gasp as he buried his shaft deep inside her.

He stayed still for endlessly long seconds, and she felt him swell, then he began to withdraw, slowly, before plunging even more deeply, repeating the action and the tempo of his rhythm until she went up in flames.

The long, slow after-play, his expertise, the wicked treachery of skilful fingers, the erotic mouth, combined to bring her to the brink and hold her there until she begged for release—and she was unsure at the peak of ecstasy whether she loved or *hated* him for what he could do to her.

Good sex. Very good sex. That's all it was, she reflected sadly as she slid through the veils of sleep.

CHAPTER TWO

'Vogel on line two.'

Gabbi's office was located high in an inner city architectural masterpiece and offered a panoramic view beyond the smoke-tinted glass exterior.

It was a beautiful summer morning, the sky a clear azure, with the sun's rays providing a dappled effect on the harbour. A Manly-bound ferry cleaved a smooth path several kilometres out from the city terminal and vied with small pleasure craft of varying sizes, all of which were eclipsed by a huge tanker heading slowly into port.

With a small degree of reluctance Gabbi turned back to her desk and picked up the receiver to deal with the call.

Five minutes later she replaced it, convinced no woman should have to cross verbal swords with an arrogant, *sexist* male whose sole purpose in life was to undermine a female contemporary.

Coffee, hot, sweet and strong, seemed like a good idea, and she rose to her feet, intent on fetching it herself rather than have her secretary do it for her. There were several files she needed to check, and she extracted the pertinent folders and laid them on her desk.

The private line beeped, and she reached for the receiver, expecting to hear James's or Benedict's voice. A lesser possibility was Marie and—even more remote—Monique.

'Gabbi.' The soft, feminine, breathy sound was unmistakable.

'Annaliese,' she acknowledged with a sinking feeling.

'Care to do lunch?'

Delaying the invitation would do no good at all, and she spared her appointment diary a quick glance. 'I can meet you at one.' She named an exclusive restaurant close by. 'Will you make the reservation, or shall I?'

'You do it, Gabbi,' Annaliese replied in a bored drawl. 'I have a meeting with my agent. I could be late.'

'I have to be back in my office at two-thirty,' Gabbi warned.

'In that case, give me ten minutes' grace, then go ahead and order.'

Gabbi replaced the receiver, had her secretary make the necessary reservation, fetched her coffee, then gave work her undivided attention until it was time to freshen up before leaving the building.

The powder-room mirror reflected an elegant image. Soft cream designer-label suit in a lightweight, uncrushable linen mix, and a silk camisole in matching tones. Her French pleat didn't need attention, and she added a touch of powder, a re-application of lipstick, then she was ready.

Ten minutes later Gabbi entered the restaurant foyer where she was greeted warmly by the maître d' and personally escorted to a table. She ordered mineral water and went through the motions of perusing the menu, opting for a Caesar salad with fresh fruit to follow.

Three-quarters of an hour after the appointed time Annaliese joined her in a waft of exclusive perfume. A slinky slither of red silk accentuated her model-slender curves. She was tall, with long slim legs, and her skilfully applied make-up enhanced her exotic features, emphasised by dark hair styled into a sleek bob.

No apology was offered, and Gabbi watched in silence as Annaliese ordered iced water, a garden salad and fresh fruit.

'When is your next assignment?'

A feline smile tilted the edges of her red mouth, and the dark eyes turned to liquid chocolate. 'So keen to see me gone?'

'A polite enquiry,' she responded with gentle mockery.

'Followed by an equally polite query regarding my career?'

Gabbi knew precisely how her stepsister's modelling career was progressing. Monique never failed to relay, in intricate detail, the events monitoring Annaliese's rise and rise on the world's catwalks.

'It was you who initiated lunch.' She picked up her glass and took a deliberate sip, then replaced it down on the table, her eyes remarkably level as she met those of her stepsister.

Annaliese's gaze narrowed with speculative contemplation. 'We've never been friends.'

In private, the younger girl had proven herself to

be a vindictive vixen. 'You worked hard to demolish any bond.'

One shoulder lifted with careless elegance. 'I wanted centre stage in our shared family, darling. *Numero uno*.' One long, red-lacquered nail tapped a careless tattoo against the stem of her glass.

Gabbi speared the last portion of cantaloupe on her plate. 'Suppose you cut to the chase and explain your purpose?'

Annaliese's eyes held a calculated gleam. 'Monique informed me James is becoming increasingly anxious for you to complete the deal.'

The fresh melon was succulent, but it had suddenly lost its taste. 'Which deal are we discussing?'

'The necessary Stanton-Nicols heir.'

Gabbi's gaze was carefully level as she rested the fork down onto her plate. 'You're way out of line, Annaliese.'

'Experiencing problems, darling?' The barb was intentional.

'Only with your intense interest in something that is none of your business.'

'It's *family* business,' Annaliese responded with deliberate emphasis.

Respect for the restaurant's fellow patrons prevented Gabbi from tipping a glass of iced water into her stepsister's lap.

'Really?' Confrontation was the favoured option. 'I have difficulty accepting my father would enrol you as messenger in such a personal matter.'

'You disbelieve me?'

'Yes.' The price of bravery might be high. Too high?

'Darling.' The word held a patronising intonation that implied the antithesis of affection. 'The only difference between daughter and stepdaughter is a legal adoption decree. Something,' she continued after a deliberate silence, 'Monique could easily persuade James to initiate.'

Oh, my. Now why didn't that devious plan surprise her? 'James's will is watertight. Monique inherits the principal residence, art and jewellery, plus a generous annuity. Shares in Stanton-Nicols come directly to me.'

One delicate brow arched high. 'You think I don't know that?' She lifted a fork and picked at her salad. 'You've missed the point.'

No, she hadn't. 'Benedict.'

Annaliese's eyes assumed an avaricious gleam. 'Clever of you, darling.'

'You want to be his mistress.'

Her soft, tinkling laugh held no humour. 'His wife.'

'You aim high.'

'The top, sweetheart.'

Iced water or hot coffee? Either was at her disposal, and she was sorely tempted to initiate an embarrassing incident. 'There's just one problem. He's already taken.'

'But so easily freed,' her stepsister purred.

'You sound very sure.' How was it possible to sound so calm, when inside she was a molten mass of fury?

'A wealthy man wants an exemplary hostess in the

lounge and a whore in his bedroom.' Annaliese examined her perfectly lacquered nails, then shot Gabbi a direct look. 'I can't imagine *passion* being your forte, or adventure your sexual preference.'

Gabbi didn't blink so much as an eyelash. 'I'm a quick study.'

'Really, darling? I wonder why I don't believe you?'

Gabbi summoned the waiter, requested the bill, and signed the credit slip. Then she rose to her feet and slid the strap of her bag over her shoulder.

'Shall we agree not to do this again?'

'Darling,' the young model almost purred. 'I'm between seasons, and where better to take in some rest and relaxation than one's home city?' Her eyes gleamed with satisfaction. 'As family, we're bound to see quite a lot of each other. The social scene is *so* interesting.'

'And you intend being included in every invitation,' Gabbi responded with soft mockery.

'Of course.'

There wasn't a single word she wanted to add. A contradiction—there were several...not one of which was in the least ladylike, and therefore unutterable in a public arena. It was easier to leave in dignified silence.

Three messages were waiting for her on her return. Two were business-oriented and she dealt with each, then logged the necessary notations into the computer before crossing to the private phone.

There was a strange curling sensation in the pit of her stomach as she waited for Benedict to answer.

'Nicols.'

His voice was deep and retained a slight American drawl that seemed more noticeable over the phone. The sound of it caused her pulse to accelerate to a faster beat.

'You rang while I was out.'

She had a mental image of him easing his lengthy frame in the high-backed leather chair. 'How was lunch?'

Her fingers gripped the receiver more tightly. 'Is there anything you don't know?'

'Annaliese requested your extension number.' He relayed the information with imperturbable calm.

Any excuse to have contact with Benedict; Gabbi silently derided her stepsister.

'You didn't answer my question.' His voice held a tinge of cynicism and prompted a terse response.

'Lunch was fine.' She drew a deep breath. 'Is that why you rang?'

'No. To let you know I won't be home for dinner. A Taiwanese associate wants to invest in property, and has requested I recommend a reputable agent. It would be impolite not to effect the introduction over dinner.'

'Very impolite,' she agreed solemnly. 'I won't wait up.'

'I'll take pleasure in waking you,' he mocked gently, ending the call.

A tiny shiver slithered the length of her spine as she recalled numerous occasions when the touch of his lips had woken her from the depths of sleep, and how she'd instinctively welcomed him, luxuriating in the agility of his hands as they traversed a tactile path over the slender curves of her body.

With concentrated effort she replaced the receiver down onto the handset, then focused her attention on work for what remained of the afternoon.

It was almost five-thirty when she left the building, and although traffic was heavy through the inner city it had begun to ease when she reached Rushcutter's Bay, resulting in a relatively clear run to Vaucluse.

The sun's rays were hot, the humidity level high. Too high, Gabbi reflected as she garaged the car and entered the house.

A long, cool drink, followed by a few lengths in the pool, would ease the strain of the day, she decided as she slipped off her jacket and made her way towards the kitchen.

Marie was putting the finishing touches to a cold platter, and her smile was warm as she watched Gabbi extract a glass and cross to the large refrigerator.

'Are you *sure* all you want is salad?'

Gabbi pushed the ice-maker lever, filled the glass with apple juice, then crossed to perch on one of four buffet stools lining the wide servery.

'Sure,' Gabbi confirmed as she leaned forward and filched a slice of fresh mango from the tastefully decorated bed of cos lettuce, avocado, nuts, and capsicum. 'Lovely,' she sighed blissfully.

Marie cast her an affectionate glance. 'There's fresh fruit and *gelato* to follow.'

Gabbi took a long swallow of iced juice, and felt the strain of the day begin to ebb. 'I think I'll change and have a swim.' The thought of a few laps in the pool followed by half an hour basking in the warm sunshine held definite appeal. 'Why don't you finish up here? There's no need for you to stay on just to rinse a few plates and stack them in the dishwasher.'

'Thanks.' The housekeeper's pleasure was evident, and Gabbi reciprocated with an impish grin.

It wasn't the first evening she'd spent alone, and was unlikely to be the last. 'Go,' she instructed. 'I'll see you at breakfast in the morning.'

Marie removed her apron and folded it neatly. 'Serg and I'll be in the flat, if you need us.'

'I know,' Gabbi said gently, grateful for the older woman's solicitous care.

Minutes later she drained the contents of her glass, then went upstairs to change, discarding her clothes in favour of a black bikini. Out of habit she removed her make-up, applied sunscreen cream, then she caught up a multi-patterned silk sarong and a towel and made her way down to the terraced pool.

Its free-form design was totally enclosed by non-reflective smoke-tinted glass, ensuring total privacy, and there were several loungers and cushioned chairs positioned on the tiled perimeters.

Gabbi dropped the sarong and towel onto a nearby chair, then performed a racing dive into the sparkling water. Seconds later she emerged to the surface, cleared excess moisture from her face, then began the first of several leisurely laps before slipping deftly onto her back to idle aimlessly for a while, enjoying the solitude and the quietness.

It was a wonderful way to relax, she mused, both mentally and physically. The cares of the day seemed to diminish to their correct perspective. Even lunch with Annaliese.

No, she amended with a faint grimace. That was taking things a bit too far. Calculating her stepsister's next move didn't require much effort, given the social scene of the city's sophisticated élite.

Stanton-Nicols supported a number of worthy charities, and Benedict generously continued in Diandra and Conrad Nicols' tradition—astutely aware that as much business was done out of the office as in it, Gabbi concluded wryly.

The thought of facing Annaliese at one function or another over the next few weeks didn't evoke much joy. Nor did the prospect of parrying Monique's subtle hints.

Damn. The relaxation cycle was well and truly broken. With a deft movement, Gabbi rolled onto her stomach and swam to the pool's edge, hauled her slim frame onto the tiled ledge, then reached for the towel and began blotting her body.

Faced with a choice of eating indoors or by the pool, she chose the latter and carried the salad and a glass of chilled water to a nearby table.

The view out over the harbour was spectacular, and she idly watched the seascape as numerous small craft cruised the waters in a bid to make the most of the daylight-saving time.

On finishing her meal, scorning television, Gabbi made herself some coffee, selected a few glossy magazines and returned to watch the sunset, the glorious streak of orange that changed and melded into a deep pink as the sun's orb sank slowly beneath the horizon providing a soft pale reflected glow before dusk turned into darkness.

A touch on the electronic modem activated the underwater light, turning the pool a brilliant aqua-blue. Another touch lit several electric flares, and she stretched out comfortably and flipped open a magazine, scanning the glossy pages for something that might capture her interest.

An article based on the behind-the-scenes life of a prominent fashion guru provided a riveting insight, and endorsed her own view on the artificiality of a society where one was never sure whether an acquaintance was friend or foe beneath the token façade.

The publishers had seen fit to include an in-depth account by a high-class madam, who, the article revealed, had procured escorts for some of the country's rich and famous, notably politicians and visiting rock stars, for a fee that was astronomical.

Somehow the article focusing on cellulite that followed it seemed extremely prosaic, and Gabbi flipped to the travel section.

Paris. What a city for ambience and *joie de vivre.* The language, the scents, the fashion. French women possessed a certain *élan* that was unmatched anywhere else in the world. And the food! *Très magnifique,* she accorded wistfully, recalling fond memories of the time she'd spent there. For a while she'd imagined herself in love with a dashing young student whose sensual expertise had almost persuaded her into his bed. Gabbi's mouth curved into a soft smile, and her eyes danced with hidden laughter in remembrance.

'An interesting article?'

Gabbi looked up at the sound of that deep, drawling voice and saw Benedict's tall frame outlined against the screened aperture leading into the large entertainment room.

His jacket was hooked over one shoulder, and he'd already removed his tie and loosened a few buttons on his blue cotton shirt.

Her eyes still held a hint of mischief as they met his. 'I didn't realise it was that late,' she managed lightly, watching as he closed the distance between them.

'It's just after ten.' He paused at her side, and scanned the open magazine. 'Pleasant memories?'

Gabbi met his gaze, and sensed the studied watchfulness beneath the surface. 'Yes,' she said with innate honesty, and saw his eyes narrow fractionally. 'It was a long time ago, and I was very young.'

'But old enough to be enchanted by a young man's attentions,' Benedict deduced with a degree of cynical amusement. 'What was his name?'

'Jacques,' she revealed without hesitation. 'He was a romantic, and he kissed divinely. We explored the art galleries together and drank coffee at numerous sidewalk cafés. On weekends I visited the family vineyard. It was fun,' she informed him simply, reflecting on the voluble and often gregarious meals she'd shared, the vivacity and sheer camaraderie of a large extended family.

'Define "fun".'

The temptation to tease and prevaricate was very strong, but there seemed little point. 'He had a very strict *maman*,' she revealed solemnly. 'Who was intent on matching him with the daughter of a neighbouring vintner. An *Anglaise* miss, albeit a very rich one, might persuade him to live on the other side of the world.'

Amusement lurked in the depths of his eyes. 'He married the vintner's daughter?'

'Yes. His devoted *maman* despatches a letter twice a year with family news.'

'Did you love him?' The query was soft, his voice silk-smooth.

Not the way I love you. 'We were very good friends,' she said with the utmost care.

His intense gaze sent a tiny flame flaring through her veins, warming her skin and heating the central core of her femininity.

'Who parted without regret or remorse when it was time for you to leave?' Benedict prompted gently.

A winsome smile curved the edges of her mouth. 'We promised never to forget each other. For a while we exchanged poetic prose.'

'Predictably the letters became shorter and few and far between?'

'You're a terrible cynic.'

'A realist,' he corrected her with subtle remonstrance.

Gabbi closed the magazine and placed it down on a nearby table. With an elegant economy of movement she rose to her feet, caught up the sarong and secured it at her waist. 'Would you like some coffee?'

'Please.'

He turned to follow her, and the hairs on the back

of her neck prickled in awareness. She subconsciously straightened her shoulders, and forced herself to walk at a leisurely pace.

In the kitchen she crossed to the servery, methodically filled the coffee-maker with water, spooned ground beans into the filter basket, then switched on the machine.

The large kitchen was a chef's delight, with every conceivable modern appliance. A central cooking island held several hobs, and there were twin ovens, two microwaves, and a capacious refrigerator and freezer.

With considerable ease Gabbi extracted two cups and saucers, then set out milk and sugar.

'How was dinner?'

'Genuine interest, or idle conversation, Gabbi?'

Was he aware of the effect he had on her? In bed, without doubt. But out of it? Probably not, she thought sadly. Men of Benedict's calibre were more concerned with creating a financial empire than examining a relationship.

It took considerable effort to meet his lightly mocking gaze. 'Genuine interest.'

'We ate Asian food in one of the city's finest restaurants,' Benedict informed her indolently. 'The business associate was suitably impressed, and the agent will probably earn a large commission.'

'Naturally you have offered them use of the private jet, which will earn you kudos with the Taiwanese associate, who in turn will recommend you to his contemporaries,' she concluded dryly, and his lips formed a twisted smile.

'It's called taking care of business.'

'And *business* is all-important.'

'Is that a statement or a complaint?'

Her eyes were remarkably steady as she held his gaze. 'It's a well-known fact that profits have soared beyond projected estimates in the past few years. Much of Stanton-Nicols' continuing success is directly attributed to your dedicated efforts.'

'You didn't answer the question.' The words held a dangerous softness that sent a tiny shiver down her spine, and her eyes clashed with his for a few immeasurable seconds before she summoned a credible smile.

'Why would I complain?' she queried evenly, supremely conscious of the quickening pulse at the base of her throat.

'Why, indeed?' he lightly mocked. 'You have a vested interest in the family firm.'

'In more ways than one.'

His eyes narrowed fractionally. 'Elaborate.'

Gabbi didn't hedge. 'The delay in providing James with a grandchild seems to be the subject of family conjecture.'

For a brief millisecond she caught a glimpse of something that resembled anger, then it was lost beneath an impenetrable mask. 'A fact which Annaliese felt compelled to bring to your attention?'

One finger came to rest against the corner of her mouth, while his thumb traced the heavy, pulsing cord at the side of her throat.

'Yes.'

His hand trailed lower to the firm swell of her

breast, teased a path along the edge of her bikini top, then brushed against the aroused peak before dropping back to his side.

'We agreed birth control should be your prerogative,' Benedict declared with unruffled ease, and she swallowed painfully, hating the way her body reacted to his touch.

'Your stepsister is too self-focused not to take any opportunity to initiate a verbal game of thrust and parry. Who won?'

'We each retired with superficial wounds,' Gabbi declared solemnly.

'Dare I ask when the game is to continue?'

'Who can tell?'

'And the weapon?'

She managed a smile. 'Why—Annaliese herself. With *you* as the prize. Her formal adoption by James would make her a *Stanton*. Our divorce is a mere formality in order to change Stanton to *Nicols*.'

He lifted a hand and brushed light fingers across her cheek. 'Am I to understand you are not impressed with that scenario?'

No. For a moment she thought she'd screamed the negative out loud, and she stood in mesmerised silence for several seconds, totally unaware that her expressive features were more explicit than any words.

'Do you believe,' Benedict began quietly, 'I deliberately chose you as my wife with the future of Stanton-Nicols foremost in mind?'

Straight for the jugular. Gabbi had expected no less. Her chin tilted slightly. 'Suitable marriages are manipulated among the wealthy for numerous reasons,' she said fearlessly. '*Love* isn't a necessary prerequisite.'

His expression didn't change, but she sensed a degree of anger and felt chilled by it.

'And what we share in bed? How would you define that?'

A lump rose in her throat, and she swallowed it. 'Skilled expertise.'

Something dark momentarily hardened the depths of his gaze, then it was gone. 'You'd relegate me to the position of *stud*?'

Oh, God. She closed her eyes, then opened them again. 'No. *No*,' she reiterated, stricken by his deliberate interpretation.

'I should be thankful for that small mercy.'

He was angry. Icily so. And it hurt, terribly.

Yet what had she expected? A heartfelt declaration that *she* was too important in his life for him to consider anyone taking her place?

Gabbi felt as if she couldn't breathe. Her eyes were trapped by his, her body transfixed as though in a state of suspended animation.

'The coffee has finished filtering.'

His voice held that familiar cynicism, and with an effort she focused her attention on pouring coffee into both cups, then added sugar.

Benedict picked up one. 'I'll take this through to the study.'

Her eyes settled on his broad back as he walked from the kitchen, her expression pensive.

Damn Annaliese, Gabbi cursed silently as she discarded her coffee down the sink. With automatic movements she rinsed the cup and stacked it in the dishwasher, then she switched off the coffee-maker and doused the lights before making her way upstairs.

Reaching the bedroom, she walked through to the *en suite*, stripped off her bikini, turned on the water and stepped into the shower.

It didn't take long to shampoo her hair, and fifteen minutes with the blow-drier restored it to its usual silky state.

In bed, she reached for a book and read a chapter before switching off the lamp.

She had no idea what time Benedict slid in beside her, nor did she sense him leave the bed in the early-morning hours, for when she woke she was alone and the only signs of his occupation were a dented pillow and the imprint of his body against the sheet.

CHAPTER THREE

GABBI glanced at the bedside clock and gave an inaudible groan. Seven-thirty. Time to rise and shine, hit the shower, breakfast, and join the queue of traffic heading into the city.

Thank heavens today was Friday and the weekend lay ahead.

Benedict had accepted an invitation to attend a tennis evening which Chris Evington, head partner in the accountancy firm Stanton-Nicols employed, had arranged at his home. Tomorrow evening they had tickets to the Australian première performance at the Sydney Entertainment Centre.

The possibility of Annaliese discovering their plans for tonight was remote, Gabbi decided as she slid in behind the wheel of her car. And it was doubtful even Monique would be able to arrange an extra seat for the première performance at such short notice.

It was a beautiful day, the sky clear of cloud, and at this early-morning hour free from pollution haze.

Gabbi was greeted by Security as she entered the car park, acknowledged at Reception *en route* to her office, and welcomed by her secretary who brought coffee in one hand and a notebook in the other.

As the morning progressed Gabbi fought against giving last night's scene too much thought, and failed.

During the afternoon she overlooked a miscalculation and lost valuable time in cross-checking. Consequently, it was a relief to slip behind the wheel of her car and head home.

Benedict's vehicle was already parked in the garage when she arrived, and she felt her stomach clench with unbidden nerves as she entered the house.

Gabbi checked with Marie, then went upstairs to change.

Benedict was in the process of discarding his tie when she reached the bedroom.

'You're home early.' As a greeting it lacked originality, but it was better than silence.

She met his dark gaze with equanimity, her eyes lingering on the hard planes of his face, and settling briefly on his mouth. Which was a mistake.

'Dinner will be ready at six.'

'So Marie informed me.' He began unbuttoning his shirt, and her eyes trailed the movement, paused, then returned to scan his features.

Nothing there to determine his mood. Damn. She hated friction. With Monique and Annaliese it was unavoidable—but Benedict was something else.

'I should apologise.' There, it wasn't hard at all. Did he know she'd summoned the courage, wrestled with the need to do so, for most of the day?

A faint smile tugged at the edges of his mouth, and the expression in his eyes was wholly cynical. 'Good manners, Gabbi?'

He shrugged off the business shirt, reached for a dark-coloured open-necked polo shirt and tugged it over his head.

Honesty was the only way to go. 'Genuine remorse.'

He removed his trousers and donned a casual cotton pair.

He looked up, and she caught the dark intensity of his gaze. 'Apology accepted.'

Her nervous tension dissolved, and the breath she'd unconsciously been holding slipped silently free. 'Thank you.'

Retreat seemed a viable option and she crossed to the capacious walk-in wardrobe, selected tennis gear, then extracted casual linen trousers and a blouse.

The buzz of the electric shaver sounded from the *en suite* bathroom, and he emerged as she finished changing.

Gabbi felt the familiar flood of warmth, and fought against it. 'What time do you want to leave?' It was amazing that her voice sounded so calm.

'Seven-fifteen.'

They descended the stairs together, and ate the delectable chicken salad Marie had prepared, washed it down with mineral water, then picked from a selection of fresh fruit. A light meal which would be supplemented by supper after the last game of tennis.

Conversation was confined to business and the proposed agenda at the next board meeting.

Chris and Leanne Evington resided at Woollahra in a large, rambling old home which had been lovingly restored. Neat lawns, beautiful gardens, precisely clipped hedges and shrubbed topiary lent an air of a past era. The immaculate grassed tennis court merely added to the impression.

A few cars lined the circular forecourt, and Gabbi slid from the Bentley as Benedict retrieved their sports bags from the boot.

Social tennis took on rules of its own, according to the host's inclination and the number of participating guests.

The best of seven games would ensure a relatively quick turn-around on the court, Chris and Leanne determined. Partners were selected by personal choice, and it was accepted that two rounds of mixed doubles would precede two rounds of women's doubles and conclude with two rounds of men's doubles.

Gabbi and Benedict were nominated first on the court, opposing a couple whom Gabbi hadn't previously met. All four were good players, although Benedict had the height, strength and skill to put the ball where he chose, and they emerged victorious at the end of the game with a five-two lead.

Chris and Leanne's son Todd had nominated himself umpire for the evening. A prominent athlete and law student, he had any number of pretty girls beating a path to his door. That there wasn't one in evidence this evening came as something of a surprise.

Until Annaliese arrived on the scene, looking sensational in designer tennis wear.

'Sorry I'm late.' Annaliese offered a winning smile.

'Mixed has just finished,' Leanne informed her. 'The girls are on next.'

Annaliese turned towards Gabbi. 'Will you be my partner? It'll be just like the old days.'

What old days? Gabbi queried silently. Surely

Annaliese wasn't referring to an occasional mismatch during school holidays?

Leanne allocated the pair to the second round, and Gabbi accepted a cool drink from a proffered tray.

The guests reassembled as Todd directed play from the umpire's seat. The men gravitated into two groups, and in no time at all Annaliese had managed to gain Gabbi's attention.

'I had a wonderful afternoon phoning friends and catching up on all their news.'

'One of whom just happened to mention the Evington tennis party?' Gabbi queried dryly.

'Why, *yes*.'

'Who better to know the guest list than Todd?'

'He's a sweet boy.'

'And easily flattered.'

Annaliese's smile was pure feline. 'Aren't most men?'

'Shall we join the others?'

It was thirty minutes before they took their position on the court, and evenly matched opponents ensured a tight score. Deuce was called three times in the final game before Annaliese took an advantage to winning point by serving an ace.

An elaborate seafood supper was provided at the close of the final game, followed by coffee and a selection of delicious petits fours.

Gabbi expected Annaliese to commandeer Benedict's attention. What she didn't anticipate was an elbow jolting her arm.

It happened so quickly that she was powerless to

do anything but watch in dismayed silence as coffee spilled onto the tiled floor.

'I'm fine,' Gabbi assured Benedict as he reached her side. She bore his swift appraisal with a determined smile.

Only a splash of hot liquid was splattered on her tennis shoes, and a cloth took care of the spillage.

'You could have been burnt,' Annaliese declared with apparent concern.

'Fortunately, I wasn't.'

'Are you sure you're OK, Gabbi?' Leanne queried. 'Can I get you some more coffee?' Her eyes took on a tinge of humour. 'Something stronger?'

She was tempted, but not for the reason her hostess imagined. A ready smile curved her mouth and she shook her head. 'Thanks all the same.'

It was almost midnight when she slid into the passenger seat of the Bentley. Benedict slipped in behind the wheel and activated the ignition.

'What happened in there?'

The car wheels crunched on the pebbled driveway, and Gabbi waited until they gained the road before responding.

'Could you be specific?'

He shot her a quick glance that lost much of its intensity in the darkness. 'You're not given to clumsiness.'

'Ah, *support*.'

'Annaliese?'

Tiredness settled like a mantle around her slim shoulders. Indecision forced a truthful answer. 'I don't know.'

'She was standing beside you.'

'I'd rather not discuss it.'

Gabbi was first indoors while Benedict garaged the car, and she went upstairs, stripped off her clothes and stepped into the shower-stall.

A few minutes later Benedict joined her, and she spared him a brief glance before continuing her actions with the soap. They each finished at the same time, emerged together and reached for individual towels.

Ignoring Benedict, especially a naked Benedict, was impossible, and there was nothing she could do to slow the quickened beat of her heart or prevent the warmth that crept through her body as she conducted her familiar nightly ritual.

A hand closed over her arm as she turned towards the door, and she didn't utter a word as he pulled her round to face him.

Eyes that were dark and impossibly slumberous held her own and she bore his scrutiny in silence, hating her inner fragility as she damned her inability to hide it.

More than anything she wanted the comfort of his arms, the satisfaction of his mouth on her own. Slowly she lifted a hand and traced the vertical indentation slashing his cheek, then pressed her fingers to the edge of his lips.

Her eyes flared as he took her fingers into his mouth, and heat unfurled deep inside her as he gently bit the tip of each finger in turn.

Unbidden, she reached for him, drawing him close, exulting in the feel of his body, his warm, musky scent, and she opened her mouth in generous acceptance of his in a deep, evocative kiss that hardened in irrefutable possession, wiping out any vestige of conscious thought.

Gabbi gave a husky purr of pleasure as he drew her into the bedroom and pulled her down onto the bed, lost in the sensual magic only he could evoke.

If business commitments didn't intrude, Benedict elected to spend Saturdays on the golf course, while Gabbi preferred to set the day aside to catch up on a variety of things a working week allowed little time for.

Occasionally she took in a matinée movie, or had lunch with friends.

Today she chose to add a few purchases to her wardrobe and keep an appointment with a beautician and her hairdresser.

Consequently it was almost six when she turned into their residential street and followed Benedict's four-wheel drive down the driveway.

He was waiting for her as she brought the car to a halt.

'Great day?' Gabbi asked teasingly as she emerged from behind the wheel.

'Indeed. And you?'

'I flashed plastic in a few too many boutiques,' she said ruefully, indicating several brightly assorted carrier bags on the rear seat.

He looked relaxed, his height and breadth accentuated by the casual open-necked shirt that fitted snugly over his well-honed muscles.

His potent masculinity ignited a familiar response deep within her as he reached past her and gathered the purchases together.

Maybe one day he wouldn't have quite this heightened effect on her equilibrium, she thought wryly as she followed him indoors. Then a silent laugh rose and died in her throat. Perhaps in another lifetime!

It was after seven when they left for the Entertainment Centre to witness the New Jersey-born son of a menswear storekeeper, who was known to mesmerise an audience with any one of the two hundred and fifty magic illusions in his repertoire.

Gabbi adored the show. Pure escapism that numbed the logical mind with wizardry and chilled the spine.

The fact that Annaliese was nowhere in sight added to her pleasure—a feeling that was compounded the next day when Gabbi and Benedict joined friends on a luxury cruiser.

Monday promised to be busier than most, Gabbi realised within minutes of arriving at the office and liaising with her secretary.

The morning hours sped by swiftly as she fed data into the computer. Concentration was required in order to maintain a high level of accuracy, and she didn't break at all when coffee was placed on her desk.

It was after midday when Gabbi sank back against the cushioned chair and flexed her shoulders as she surveyed the computer screen. The figures were keyed in, all she had to do was run a check on them after lunch.

A working lunch, she decided, fired with determination to meet a personal deadline. James had requested the information by one o'clock tomorrow. She intended that he would have it this afternoon.

Gabbi rose from her desk, extracted the chicken salad sandwich her secretary had placed in the concealed bar fridge an hour earlier, selected a bottle of apple juice and returned to her seat.

The bread was fresh, the chicken soft on a bed of crisp salad topped with a tangy mayonnaise dressing. Washed down with juice, it replenished her energy store.

The phone rang and she hurriedly plucked free a few tissues from the box on her desk, then reached for the receiver.

'Francesca Angeletti on line one.'

Surprise was quickly followed by pleasure. 'Put her through.' Two seconds ticked by. 'Francesca. Where are you?'

'Home. I flew in from Rome yesterday morning.'

'When are we going to get together?' There was no question that they wouldn't. They had shared the same boarding-school, the same classes, and each had a stepmother. It was a common bond that had drawn them together and fostered a friendship which had extended beyond school years.

Francesca's laugh sounded faintly husky. 'Tonight, if you and Benedict are attending Leon's exhibition.'

'Leon's soirées are high on our social calendar,' she acknowledged with an answering chuckle.

'James will be there with Monique?'

'And Annaliese,' Gabbi added dryly, and one eyebrow lifted at Francesca's forthright response. 'Nice girls don't swear,' she teased in admonition.

'This one does,' came the swift reply. 'How long has your dear stepsister been disturbing your home turf?'

'A week.'

'She is fond of playing the diva,' Francesca commented. 'I had the misfortune to share a few of the same catwalks with her in Italy.'

'Fun.'

'Not the kind that makes you laugh. Gabbi, I have to dash. We'll catch up tonight, OK?'

'I'll really look forward to it,' Gabbi assured her, and replaced the receiver.

For the space of a few minutes she allowed her mind to skim the years, highlighting the most vivid of shared memories: school holidays abroad together, guest of honour at each other's engagement party, bridesmaid at each other's wedding.

The automatic back-up flashed on the computer screen, and succeeded in returning her attention to the task at hand. With determination she drew her chair forward, reached for the sheaf of papers, and systematically began checking figure columns.

An hour later she printed out, collated, then had her secretary deliver copies to James and Benedict. She was well pleased with the result. The reduction of a percentage point gained by successful negotiations with the leasing firm for Stanton-Nicols' company car fleet could be used to boost the existing employee incentive package. At no extra cost to Stanton-Nicols, and no loss of tax advantage.

It was after five when she rode the lift down to the car park and almost six when she entered the house.

'Benedict just called,' Marie informed Gabbi when she appeared in the kitchen. 'He'll be another twenty minutes.'

Time for her to shower and wash and dry her hair. 'Smells delicious,' she complimented as she watched Marie deftly stir the contents of one saucepan, then tend to another.

'Asparagus in a hollandaise sauce, beef Wellington with vegetables and lemon tart for dessert.'

Gabbi grabbed a glass and crossed to the refrigerator for some iced water.

'A few invitations arrived in the mail. They're in the study.'

'Thanks,' she said, smiling.

A few minutes later she ran lightly up the stairs, and in the bedroom she quickly discarded her clothes then made for the shower.

Afterwards she donned fresh underwear, pulled on fitted jeans and a loose top, then twisted her damp hair into a knot on top of her head. A quick application of moisturiser, a light touch of colour to her lips and she was ready.

Benedict entered the bedroom as she emerged from the *en suite*, and she met his mocking smile with a deliberate slant of one eyebrow.

'A delayed meeting?'

'Two phone calls and a traffic snarl,' he elaborated as he shrugged off his jacket and loosened his tie.

She moved towards the door. 'Dinner will be ready in ten minutes.'

The gleam in those dark eyes was wholly sensual. 'I had hoped to share your shower.'

Something tugged at her deep inside, flared, then spread throughout her body. 'Too late,' she declared lightly as she drew level with him.

His smile widened, accentuating the vertical lines slashing each cheek. 'Shame.'

Her breath rose unsteadily in her throat as she attempted to still the rapid beat of her pulse. Did he take pleasure in deliberately teasing her?

'A cool shower might help.'

'So might this.' He reached for her, angling his mouth down over hers in a kiss that held the promise of passion and the control to keep it at bay.

Gabbi felt her composure waver, then splinter and fragment as he drew deeply, taking yet giving, until she surrendered herself to the evocative pleasure only he could provide.

A tiny moan sounded low in her throat as he slowly raised his head, and she swayed slightly, her eyes wide, luminous pools as she surveyed his features. Her breathing was rapid, her skin warm, and her mouth trembled as she drew back from his grasp.

'You don't play fair,' she accused him shakily, and stood still as he brushed the backs of his fingers across her cheek.

His lips curved, the corners lifting in a semblance of lazy humour. 'Go check with Marie,' he bade her gently. 'I'll be down soon.'

Dinner was superb, the asparagus tender, the beef succulent and the lemon tart an excellent finale.

'Coffee?' Marie asked as she packed dishes onto a trolley.

Gabbi spared her watch a quick glance. It would take thirty minutes to dress, apply make-up and style her hair. 'Not for me.'

'Thanks, Marie. Black,' Benedict requested as Gabbi rose from the table.

CHAPTER FOUR

GABBI chose red silk evening trousers, matching camisole and beaded jacket. It was a striking outfit, complete with matching evening sandals and clutch-purse. The colour enhanced her delicate honey-coloured skin, and provided an attractive contrast for her blonde hair.

With extreme care she put the finishing touches to her make-up, donned the trousers and camisole, then brushed her hair. Loose, she decided, after sweeping it high and discarding the customary French pleat.

Her mirrored image revealed a confident young woman whose clothes and jewellery bore the exclusivity of wealth. There was a coolness to her composure, a serenity she was far from feeling.

Which proved just how deceptive one's appearance could be, she decided wryly as she slid her feet into the elegant sandals.

'Is the colour choice deliberate?'

'Why do you ask?' Gabbi countered as she met Benedict's indolent gaze.

'I get the impression you're bent on making a statement,' he drawled, and she directed a deceptively sweet smile at him.

'How perceptive of you.'

He looked the epitome of male sophistication, the

dark evening suit a stark contrast to the white cotton shirt and black bow tie.

It was almost a sin, she reflected, for any one man to exude such a degree of sexual chemistry. The strong angles and planes of his facial features bore the stamp of his character. The unwavering eyes were hard and inflexible in the boardroom, yet they filled with brooding passion in the bedroom. And the promise of his mouth was to die for, she concluded, all too aware of the havoc it could cause.

He possessed the aura of a predator, arresting and potentially dangerous. Compelling, she added silently.

A tiny thrill of excitement quivered deep inside her at the thought of the pleasure it would give her to pull his tie free and help discard his clothes. And have him remove her own.

'Why the faint smile?'

The desire to shock deepened the smile and lent her eyes a tantalising sparkle. 'Anticipation,' she enlightened him wickedly.

'Of Leon's exhibition?'

She doubted he was fooled in the slightest, for he seemed to find her achingly transparent. 'Naturally.'

'We could always arrive late,' Benedict suggested in dry, mocking tones, and the edges of her mouth formed a delicious curve.

'Leon would be disappointed.' Not to mention Annaliese, she added silently, mentally weighing up which might be the worst offence.

'I could always placate him by making an exorbitant purchase.'

She gave it consideration, then shook her head with apparent reluctance.

'Teasing incurs a penalty,' Benedict declared with soft emphasis.

'I am suitably chastened.'

'That compounds with every hour,' he completed silkily, and saw the momentary flicker of uncertainty cloud those beautiful eyes. It made him want to reach out and touch his hand to her cheek, see the uncertainty fade as he bent his head to claim her mouth. He succumbed to the first but passed on the latter.

Gabbi collected her clutch-purse and preceded him from the room, and, seated inside the Jaguar, she remained silent, aware that the latent power of the sports car equalled that of the man seated behind the wheel.

To attempt to play a game with him, even an innocuous one, was foolish, she perceived as the car purred along the suburban streets. For even when she won she really lost. It didn't seem quite fair that he held such an enormous advantage. Yet the likelihood of tipping the scales in her favour seemed incredibly remote.

'How did James react to your proposal?' Business was always a safe subject.

Benedict turned his head slightly and directed a brief glance at her before focusing his attention on the road. 'Small talk, Gabbi?'

'I can ask James,' she responded steadily.

'I fly to Melbourne in a couple of weeks.'

I, not *we*, she thought dully. 'How long will you be away?'

'Three, maybe four days.'

She should have been used to his frequent trips interstate and overseas. Yet she felt each absence more keenly than the last, intensely aware of her own vulnerability, *and*, dammit, incredibly insecure emotionally.

Gabbi wanted to say she'd miss him, but that would be tantamount to an admission she wasn't prepared to make. Instead, she focused her attention on the scene beyond the windscreen, noting the soft haze that had settled over the city, the azure, pink-fringed sky as the sun sank beyond the horizon. Summer daylight-time delayed the onset of dusk, but soon numerous street-lamps would provide a fairy tracery of light, and the city would be lit with flashing neon.

The views were magnificent: numerous coves and inlets, the grandeur of the Opera House against the backdrop of Harbour Bridge. It was a vista she took for granted every day as she drove to work, and now she examined it carefully, aware that the plaudits acclaiming it one of the most attractive harbours in the world were well deserved.

Traffic at this hour was relatively minimal, and they reached Double Bay without delay. There was private parking adjacent to the gallery, and Benedict brought the Jaguar to a smooth halt in an empty bay.

Gabbi released the door-latch and slid out of the passenger seat, resisting the urge to smooth suddenly nervous fingers over the length of her hair. It was merely another evening in which she was required to smile and converse and pretend that everything was as it appeared to be.

She'd had a lot of practice, she assured herself silently as she walked at Benedict's side to the entrance.

The gallery held an interesting mix of patrons, Gabbi could see as she preceded Benedict into the elegant foyer.

Their presence elicited an ebullient greeting from the gallery owner, whose flamboyant dress style and extravagant jewellery were as much an act as was his effusive manner. A decade devoted to creating an image and fostering clientele had paid off, for his *'invitation only'* soirées were considered *de rigueur* by the city's social élite.

'Darlings, how are we, *ça va*?'

Gabbi accepted the salutatory kiss on each cheek and smiled at the shrewd pair of eyes regarding her with affection.

'Leon,' she responded quietly, aware that the Italian-born Leo had acknowledged his French roots after discovering his ancestors had fled France during the French Revolution. 'Well, *merci.*'

'That is good.' He caught hold of Benedict's hand and pumped it enthusiastically. 'There are some *wonderful* pieces. At least one I'm sure will be of immense interest. I shall show it to you personally. But first some champagne, *oui*?' He beckoned a hovering waiter and plucked two flutes from the tray, then commanded a uniformed waitress to bring forth a selection of hors d'oeuvres. 'Beluga, smoked salmon, anchovy.'

Gabbi selected a thin wafer artfully decorated with smoked salmon topped with a cream cheese and caper dressing. 'Delicious,' she complimented. 'Franz has excelled himself.'

'Thank you, darling,' Leon said gently. 'Now, do mingle. You already know almost everyone. I'll be back with you later.'

She moved forward, conscious of the interest their presence aroused. It was definitely smile-time, and she greeted one fellow guest after another with innate charm, pausing to indulge in idle chatter before moving on.

How long would it be before James made an entrance with Monique on one arm and Annaliese on the other? Ten, fifteen minutes?

Twenty, Gabbi acknowledged when she caught sight of her father, caught his smile and returned it as he threaded his way through the throng of guests.

'Hello, darling.' He squeezed her hand, then turned to greet his son-in-law. 'Benedict.'

'Monique.' Gabbi went through with the air-kiss routine. 'Annaliese.'

Her stepsister's perfume was subtle. Her dress, however, was not. Black, it fitted Annaliese's slender curves like a glove, the hemline revealing an almost obscene length of long, smooth thigh and highlighting the absence of a bra.

There wasn't a red-blooded man in the room whose eyes didn't momentarily gleam with appreciation. Nor was there a woman in doubt of her man who didn't fail to still the slither of alarm at the sight of this feline female on the prowl.

Gabbi could have assured each and every one of

them that their fears were unfounded. Benedict was the target, *she* the victim.

'Have you seen anything you like?'

To anyone overhearing the enquiry, it sounded remarkably genuine. Gabbi, infinitely more sensitive, recognised the innuendo in Annaliese's voice and searched for it in Benedict's reply.

'Yes. One or two pieces have caught my interest.'

'Are you going to buy?' asked Monique, intrigued, yet able to portray dispassionate detachment.

Gabbi doubted if James was aware of his step-daughter's machinations, or her collusion with his wife.

'Possibly,' Benedict enlightened her smoothly.

'You must point them out to me,' Annaliese purred in a voice filled with seductive promise.

Gabbi wanted to hit her. For a wild second she envisaged the scene and drew satisfaction from a mental victory.

'Numbers five and thirty-seven,' Benedict was informing Annaliese.

'Gabbi, why don't you take Monique and Annaliese on a tour of the exhibits?' James suggested. 'I have something I'd like to discuss with Benedict.'

Oh, my. Did her father realise he'd just thrown her to the lions?

'The girls can go,' Monique said sweetly. 'I'll have a word with Bertrice Osterman.'

How opportune for one of the society doyennes to be within close proximity. Gabbi offered Annaliese a faint smile. 'Shall we begin?'

It took two minutes and something like twenty

paces to reach Benedict's first choice. 'It leans towards the avant garde,' Gabbi declared. 'But it will brighten up one of the office walls.'

'Cut the spiel, Gabbi,' Annaliese said in bored tones. 'These art exhibitions are the pits.'

'But socially stimulating, wouldn't you agree?'

'Monique came along to be seen, and—'

'So did you,' Gabbi interceded quietly.

'By Benedict.'

She felt the breath catch in her throat, and willed her expression not to change.

'Surely you didn't doubt it, darling?'

'I expected nothing less,' she managed civilly.

'Then we understand each other.'

Gabbi extended a hand towards a row of paintings. 'Shall we pretend to look at the other exhibits?' She even managed a credible smile. 'It will provide you with a topic of conversation.'

Annaliese was, Gabbi conceded, a consummate actress. No one in the room would guess there was no love lost between the two stepsisters. And Gabbi hated participating in the façade.

For fifteen minutes they wandered, paused and examined, before rejoining James and Benedict. Monique was nowhere in sight.

'Wonderful choice, Benedict,' Annaliese said in a deliberately throaty tone. 'There's a sculpture that would look incredible in the corner of your office. You must come and see it.' She turned towards Gabbi. 'It is quite spectacular, isn't it, darling?'

'Spectacular,' Gabbi conceded, taking a fresh flute of champagne from the tray proffered by a waiter. She lifted the glass to her lips and took a pensive sip, then dared to raise her eyes to meet those of her husband. They were dark and faintly brooding, with just a tinge of latent humour. He was amused, damn him!

'Then I shall have to take a look.'

'Talk to James, darling, while I drag Benedict away.'

It was a beautiful manoeuvre, Gabbi applauded silently as Annaliese drew Benedict across the room.

'She's grown into a very attractive girl,' James said quietly, and Gabbi inclined her head.

'Very attractive,' she agreed solemnly.

'Incredibly successful, too.'

'Yes.' She took a careful sip of champagne and steeled herself not to glance towards where Annaliese held Benedict's attention.

'I looked at those figures you submitted. They're excellent.'

'Thank you,' she accepted, pleased at his praise.

'You possess your mother's integrity, her sense of style,' he said gently. 'I'm very proud of you, Gabbi. And of what you've achieved.'

She brushed a quick kiss over his cheek. 'I love you too.'

'James.'

Gabbi turned at the sound of an unfamiliar voice, smiled, and stood quietly as her father completed an introduction. A business associate who seemed intent on discussing the effects of an upcoming state election. With a murmured excuse, she left the two men to converse and began threading her way towards the opposite side of the room.

There were quite a few people present whom she knew, and she paused to exchange greetings.

A painting had caught her eye shortly after they'd arrived, and she wanted to take another look at it.

'Gabbi.'

'Francesca!' Her smile was genuinely warm as she embraced the tall, svelte auburn-haired model. 'It seems ages since I last saw you.'

'Too long,' Francesca agreed. 'The catwalks were exhausting, and—' she paused fractionally '—the family daunting.'

'Do we get to talk about this over lunch?'

Francesca's smile was infectious. 'Tomorrow?'

'Love to,' Gabbi agreed, and named a fashionable restaurant a short distance from the office. 'Twelve-thirty?'

'Done.' Francesca took hold of her arm. 'Do you particularly *want* to watch Annaliese's attempt to snare Benedict?'

'No.'

'Then let's do the unexpected and examine the art exhibits for any hidden talent!' An eyebrow arched in a sardonic gesture as she cast a glance at a nearby sculpture. 'There has to be *some*, surely?'

'It's a case of beauty being in the eye of the beholder,' Gabbi vouchsafed solemnly as they moved from one painting to another.

'The prices are scandalous,' Francesca opined in a quiet aside. 'Does anyone actually make a purchase?'

'You'd be surprised.'

'Utterly.'

'Some of the city's rich and famous are known to

buy on a whim, then years later make a killing when the artist becomes well-known.'

'And if the artist doesn't?'

Gabbi smiled. 'They place it in the foyer of their office and pretend its obscure origin makes it a curiosity piece. The added advantage being the item then becomes a legitimate tax deduction.'

'Oh, my,' Francesca breathed. 'When did you become so cynical?'

'I grew up.' It shouldn't hurt so much. But it did.

'And Benedict?'

She hesitated a moment too long. 'We understand each other.'

'That's a loaded statement, darling. I rather imagined he was your knight in shining armour.'

'That myth belongs in a story book.'

'Not always,' Francesca disagreed gently. 'I experienced a brief taste of it.'

Too brief. Francesca's marriage to a world-famous Italian racing-car driver had lasted six months. A freak accident three years ago on a tight turn had claimed his life and that of another driver, the horrific scene captured for ever on news-film.

Gabbi had flown to Monaco to attend the funeral, and hadn't been able to express adequate words then, any more than she could now.

'It's OK,' Francesca said quietly, almost as if she knew. 'I'm learning to deal with it.'

Gabbi had witnessed the magic, *seen* for herself the rare depth of their shared love, and wondered if it was possible to cope with such a loss.

'Mario was—'

'One of a kind,' Francesca interrupted gently. 'For a while he was mine. At least I have that.' She pointed out a glaring canvas whose colours shrieked with vivid, bold strokes. 'Was that a kindergarten tot let loose with brush and palette, do you suppose? Or is there some mysterious but meaningful symmetry that momentarily escapes the scope of my imagination?'

'It's an abstract,' an amused male voice revealed. 'And you're looking at the kindergarten tot who took an afternoon to slash the canvas with paint in the hope someone might pay for the privilege of putting bread on my table.'

'Expensive bread,' Francesca remarked without missing a beat. 'The artist favours hand-stitched shoes, a Hermes tie and wears a Rolex.'

'They could be fake,' he declared.

'No,' Francesca asserted with the certainty of one who *knew* designer apparel.

Gabbi watched the interplay between her friend and the tall, broad-framed man whose dark eyes held a piercing brilliance.

'Next you'll tell me where I live and what car I drive.'

'Not what people would expect of an artist,' Francesca considered with scarcely a thought. 'Northern suburbs, overlooking water, trees in the garden, a detached studio and a BMW in the garage.'

Gabbi sensed Benedict's presence an instant before she felt the touch of firm fingers at the edge of her waist, and she summoned a dazzling smile as she turned slightly towards him.

The eyes that lanced hers were dark and impossible to fathom so she didn't even try.

'Benedict,' Francesca greeted him warmly. 'It's been a while.'

'Indeed,' he agreed urbanely. 'You've met Dominic?'

'We haven't been formally introduced.' Francesca's smile was deliberately warm as she turned her head towards the man at her side.

'Dominic Andrea. Entrepreneur and part-time artist,' Benedict informed her. 'Francesca Angeletti.'

'How opportune. The designer luggage won't require a change of initials.'

Gabbi registered Dominic's words and heard Francesca's almost inaudible gasp one second ahead of Benedict's husky chuckle.

'You must come to dinner,' Dominic insisted. 'Bring Francesca.'

'Gabbi?' Benedict deferred, and she caught her breath that the decision should be hers.

'Thank you, we'd love to.'

'No,' the glamorous widow declined.

'I have yet to nominate a night,' Dominic said in mild remonstrance. 'And with Benedict and Gabbi present you'll be quite safe.' His smile was dangerously soft and filled with latent charm. 'Aren't you in the least curious to see if you're right?'

Gabbi watched Francesca's eyes narrow and heard her voice chill to ice. 'Where you live doesn't interest me.'

'Tomorrow,' he insisted gently. 'Six-thirty.' He

turned and threaded his way to the opposite side of the gallery.

'What a preposterous man,' Francesca hissed disdainfully the moment he was out of earshot.

'A very rich and successful one,' Benedict added mildly. 'Who dabbles in art and donates his work to worthwhile charities.'

'He's a friend of yours?'

'We occasionally do business together. He spends a lot of time overseas. New York, Athens, Rome,' Benedict enlightened her.

'Champagne, caviare and camaraderie aren't my style,' Francesca dismissed.

'You share something in common,' Benedict informed her with a degree of cynical amusement.

'Then why the dinner invitation?'

'He admires your charming wit,' Benedict responded wryly, and his mouth curved to form an amused smile.

'An attempt to charm wasn't my intention,' Francesca declared with an expressive lift of one eyebrow.

'Perhaps he is sufficiently intrigued to want to discover why not?' Benedict ventured in a dry undertone.

'I presume women rarely refuse him.'

A low chuckle escaped Benedict's throat. 'Rarely.'

Gabbi witnessed the faint sparkle evident in her friend's eyes, and was unable to repress a winsome smile. 'So you'll accept?'

'It's a long time since I've been offered such an interesting evening,' Francesca conceded. 'I'll let you know at lunch tomorrow.'

Benedict drew their attention to an intricate steel sculpture that was garnering a great deal of notice, and after a few minutes Francesca indicated her intention to leave.

'Do you want to stay for Leon's party?' Benedict queried minutes later, and Gabbi cast him a studied glance.

'I imagine you've already presented him with a sizeable cheque, sufficient to appease any regret he might express at our absence?' The words were lightly voiced and brought a faint smile to his lips.

'Exhibits five and thirty-seven, plus the sculpture Annaliese admired.'

A knife twisted inside her stomach.

'A gift for James,' he added with gentle mockery.

She held his gaze with difficulty, unsure what interpretation to place on his words, or if there was *any* hidden innuendo in them. 'I'm sure he'll be most appreciative,' she said after a measurable silence.

'You didn't answer my question,' Benedict reminded her gently.

'James, Monique and Annaliese have yet to leave.' It was amazing that her voice sounded so calm, equally surprising that she was able to project an outward serenity. But then she'd had plenty of practice at conveying both.

Humour tugged at the edges of his mouth. 'I was unaware that their presence, or absence, dictated our own,' he countered with deceptive mildness.

It didn't, but she hadn't quite forgiven him for being so easily led away by Annaliese or for being caught so long in conversation.

She effected a slight shrug he could interpret any way he chose. 'If you want to leave—'

'You're not going?' Monique intervened, her voice tinged with mild reproach, and Gabbi wondered if lip-reading was one of her stepmother's acquired skills. 'Leon will be most upset if you miss his party.'

'A headache,' Benedict invented smoothly.

Monique spared Gabbi a penetrating look. 'Oh darling, really?' Her eyes sharpened suspiciously.

Annaliese's mouth formed a pretty pout. 'What a shame to end the evening so early.' She turned sultry eyes towards Benedict. 'Perhaps Gabbi won't mind if you drop her home and come back for the party?'

Benedict's smile didn't quite reach his eyes. 'I'm the one who is suffering,' he informed her, subjecting Gabbi to a deliberate appraisal that left no one in any doubt that his suffering was of a sexual nature.

Monique's expression didn't change and James's features remained deliberately bland, although Gabbi thought she glimpsed a fleeting humorous twinkle in his eyes. Annaliese, however, shot her a brief, malevolent glare before masking it with a faint smile.

'Have fun,' Annaliese murmured, pressing her scarlet-tipped fingers to Benedict's arm in a light caress.

Gabbi prayed that the soft flood of warmth to her cheeks wasn't accompanied by a telling tide of pink as Benedict smoothly uttered the few necessary words in farewell, and her fingers clenched against his in silent retaliation as he caught hold of her hand and began threading his way across the room to where Leon was holding court with a captive audience.

'Oh, darlings, you're leaving?'

'You don't mind?'

'I'm so pleased you were able to attend.' Leon's smile was beatific, courtesy of Benedict's cheque in his wallet.

Gabbi waited until Benedict had steered the Jaguar clear of the car park before launching into a verbal attack.

'That was unforgivable!'

'What, precisely, did you find unforgivable?' Benedict drawled in amusement as he joined the traffic travelling eastward along the New South Head road.

She wanted to rage at him, physically *hit* him. Instead she chose to remain silent for the time it took him to reach Vaucluse, garage the car and enter the house.

'Coffee?' Benedict enquired as he turned from resetting the alarm system.

'No,' she refused tightly, raising stormy eyes to meet his as he closed the distance between them.

He made no attempt to touch her, and she stood firmly resolute, hating him for a variety of reasons that were too numerous to mention.

'So much anger,' he observed indolently.

'What did you expect?'

'A little gratitude, perhaps, for initiating a premature escape?'

Words warred with each other in her mind as she fought for control. More than anything she wanted to lash out and hit him, and only the silent warning apparent in those dark features stopped her.

'You take exception to the fact I want to make love

with you?' he queried silkily. Lifting a hand, he slid it beneath the curtain of her hair.

'I didn't expect a clichéd announcement of your intention,' she threw at him angrily, gasping as he cupped her nape and angled his head down to hers. *'Don't.'*

The plea went unheeded as his mouth closed over hers, and she strained against the strength of his arm as it curved down her back and held her to him.

Slowly, insidiously, warmth coursed through her veins until her whole body was one aching mass, craving his touch, and she opened her mouth to accept the possession of his own.

Passion replaced anger, and a tiny part of her brain registered the transition and wondered at the traitorous dictates of her own heart.

It wasn't fair that he should have quite this effect on her, or that she should have so little control. Sex motivated by lust wasn't undesired, but *love* was the ultimate prize.

She wanted to protest when he swept an arm beneath her knees and lifted her against his chest. She knew she should as he climbed the stairs to the upper floor. And when he entered their bedroom and let her slip down to her feet she stood, quiescent, as he gently removed her beaded jacket and tossed it over a nearby chair.

The soft light from twin lamps reflected against the mirror and she caught a momentary glimpse of two figures—one tall and dark, the other slender in red, then she became lost in the heat of Benedict's impassioned gaze, her fingers as dexterous as his in their quest to remove each layer of clothing.

Yet there was care apparent, almost a teasing quality as they each dealt with buttons and zip-fastenings, the slide of his hands on her exposed flesh increasing the steady spiral of excitement.

He wasn't unmoved by her ministrations either, and she exulted in the feel of tightening sinews as she caressed his muscled chest, the taut waist and the thrust of his powerful thighs.

His heartbeat quickened in tempo with her own as he pulled her down onto the bed and she rose up above him, every nerve, every *cell* alive with anticipation. She sought to give as much pleasure as she knew she'd receive, taking the path to climactic nirvana with deliberate slowness, enjoying and enhancing each step of the emotional journey until there was no sense of the individual, only the merging of two souls so in tune with each other that they became one.

And afterwards they lay, arms and legs entwined, exchanging the soft caress of fingers against warm flesh, the light, lingering brush of lips, in an after-play that held great tenderness and care, until sleep claimed them both.

CHAPTER FIVE

THE sun's rays were hot after the controlled coolness of the building's air-conditioning, and Gabbi felt the heat come up from the pavement combined with the jostle of midday city staff anxious to make the most of their lunch hour, elderly matrons *en route* from one shopping mall to another and mothers with young children in tow.

Sydney was a vibrant city alive with people from different cultures, and Gabbi witnessed a vivid kaleidoscope of couture and grunge as she walked the block and a half to meet Francesca.

The restaurant was filled with patrons, but she'd rung ahead for a reservation, and the maître d' offered an effusive greeting and ushered her to a table.

There was barely time to order iced water before Francesca slid into the opposite seat in a soft cloud of Hermes Calèche perfume.

'The traffic was every bit as bad as I expected,' Francesca commented as she ordered the same drink as Gabbi. 'And securing a parking space was worse.'

Gabbi smiled in commiseration. 'City commuting is the pits.' She picked up the menu. 'Shall we order?'

'Good idea. I'm starving,' Francesca admitted with relish, selecting the *soupe du jour* followed by a Greek salad and fresh fruit.

Gabbi also selected her friend's choice, but opted for linguini instead of soup as a starter.

'How long will you be Sydney-based?' Her smile was warm, her interest genuine.

Ice-cubes chinked as Francesca picked up her glass. 'Not long. A few weeks, then I'll head back to Europe.'

True friendship was rare, and with it came the benefit of dispensing with the niceties of idle conversation. 'So, tell me about Rome.'

Francesca's expression became pensive. 'Mario's mother was diagnosed with inoperable cancer.'

Gabbi's heart constricted with pain, and she reached out and covered her friend's hand with her own. 'Francesca, I'm so sorry.'

'We had a few short weeks together before she was hospitalised, and after that it was only a matter of days.' Francesca's eyes darkened with repressed emotion. 'She bequeathed me everything.'

'Mario was her only child,' Gabbi reminded her gently.

'Nevertheless, it was—' she paused fractionally '—unexpected.'

The waiter's appearance with their starters provided an interruption.

'What's new with the family?' Francesca asked as soon as he was out of earshot.

'Not a thing.'

'Benedict is to die for, Monique superficially gracious, Annaliese a bitch and James remains oblivious?'

The assessment was so accurate, Gabbi didn't know

whether to laugh or cry. 'Selectively oblivious,' she qualified.

'A clever man, your father.'

'And yours, Francesca?'

'Consumed with business in order to keep my dear stepmama in the incredible style she insists is important.' She managed a tight smile. 'While Mother continues to flit from one man to the next with time out in between for the requisite nip and tuck.'

They finished the starters and began on the salads.

'Dominic Andrea,' Francesca ventured speculatively. 'Greek?'

'Second generation. His mother is Australian.'

'Irritating man.'

Dominic was many things, but irritating wasn't one of them. 'Do you think so?'

'And arrogant.'

Perhaps. Although Gabbi would have substituted self-assured. 'You want to opt out of dinner tonight?'

Francesca forked the last mouthful of salad, took her time with it, then replaced the utensil onto her plate. 'No,' she said thoughtfully, her gaze startlingly direct. 'Why deny myself an interesting evening?'

Gabbi's mouth curved with humour. 'A clash between two Titans?'

Francesca's eyes assumed a speculative gleam. 'It will be an intriguing challenge to beat the man at his own game.'

Indeed, Gabbi accorded silently. Although she wasn't sure that Francesca would win.

The waiter brought a fruit platter and they ordered coffee.

'Shall I give you Dominic's address?' Gabbi queried as she picked up the bill, quelling Francesca's protest. 'Or will we collect you?'

'I'll meet you there.' She extracted a pen and paper from her handbag and took down the address. 'Six-thirty?'

'Yes,' Gabbi confirmed as they emerged out onto the pavement. She accepted Francesca's light kiss on each cheek, and touched her hand as they parted. 'It's been great to catch up. Take care.'

'Always,' Francesca promised. 'See you tonight.'

There were several messages on Gabbi's desk when she returned, and she dealt with each, dictated several letters and worked on streamlining overheads in a subsidiary company. Systematic checking was required to discover alternative suppliers who, she was convinced, could provide an equal service for a more competitive price. She made a list of relevant numbers to call.

The intercom buzzed, and Gabbi depressed the button. 'Yes, Halle?'

'There's a parcel in Reception for you. Shall I bring it down?'

She eased her shoulders and pushed a stray tendril of hair behind one ear. 'Please.'

A minute later her secretary appeared carrying a flat rectangular parcel wrapped in brown paper. 'There's an envelope. Want me to open it?'

It couldn't be...could it? Gabbi rose to her feet and crossed round to the front of her desk. 'No, I'll take care of it. Thanks, Halle.'

She placed the attached envelope on her desk, then

undid the wrapping, pleasure lighting up her features as she revealed the painting she'd admired at Leon's gallery.

It was perfect for the southern wall of her office.

The card held a simple message: 'For you.' It was signed 'Benedict.'

Gabbi reached for the private phone and punched in Benedict's coded number.

He answered on the second ring. 'Nicols.'

'You noticed my interest in the painting,' she said with evident warmth. 'I love it. Thanks.'

'Why don't you take a walk to my office and thank me in person?' The lazy drawl held mild amusement, and a soft laugh emerged from her throat.

'A momentary diversion?'

'Very momentary,' Benedict agreed with light humour. 'An associate is waiting in my private lounge.'

'In that case, you shouldn't delay seeing him,' she chastised him sweetly, and heard his husky chuckle in response.

'Tonight, Gabbi.'

She heard the faint click as he replaced the receiver.

The rest of the afternoon went quickly, and at five she shut down the computer, signed the completed letters then collected her briefcase and took the lift down to the car park.

Benedict's four-wheel drive was in the garage when she arrived home, and as they were to dine out she bypassed the kitchen and made for the stairs.

It would be nice to strip off and relax in the Jacuzzi, she thought longingly as she entered the master suite, but there wasn't time. Twenty-five minutes in which to shower, dress, apply make-up and style her hair didn't allow for a leisurely approach.

The sound of an electric razor in action could be heard from the bathroom and she quickly shed her clothes, pulled on a silk robe and pushed open the door.

Benedict was standing in front of the wide mirror dispensing with a day's growth of beard, a towel hitched at his waist. It was evident from his damp hair that he hadn't long emerged from the shower.

'Hi.' It irked her that her voice sounded vaguely breathless. Maybe in another twenty years she would be able to view his partly naked form and not feel so completely *consumed* by the sight of him.

If, that far down the track, she was still part of his life. The thought that she might not be brought a stab of unbearable pain.

He looked up from his task and met her eyes in the mirror. 'Hi, yourself.'

His appraisal was warm and lingered a little too long on the soft curve of her mouth. With determined effort she reached into the shower-stall, turned on the water, slipped off her robe and stepped beneath the warm jet-spray. When she emerged it was to find she had sole occupancy of the bathroom.

Ten minutes later her hair was swept into a sleek pleat, her make-up complete. In the bedroom she crossed to the walk-in closet and selected silk evening trousers in delicate ivory, added a beaded camisole and slid her arms into a matching silk jacket. Gold jewellery and elegant evening sandals completed the outfit, and she took time to dab her favourite perfume to a few exposed pulse-points before catching up an evening purse.

'Ready?'

With a few minutes to spare. She directed a cool glance at him. 'Yes. Shall we leave?'

Dominic's home was a brilliant example of architectural design in suburban Beauty Point overlooking the middle harbour.

Dominic greeted them at the door and drew them into the lounge.

High ceilings and floor-to-ceiling glass lent the room spaciousness and light, with folding white-painted wooden shutters and deep-cushioned furniture providing a hint of the Caribbean.

There was no sign of Francesca, and Gabbi wondered if she was deliberately planning her arrival to be a fashionable, but excusable, five minutes late.

Ten, Gabbi noted, as the bell-chimes pealed when she was partway through a delicious fruit cocktail. Dominic allowed his housekeeper to answer the door.

It would seem that if Francesca had a strategy Dominic had elected to choose one of his own.

Stunning was an apt description of Francesca's appearance, Gabbi silently applauded as she greeted her friend. Francesca's expression was carefully bland, but there was a wicked twinkle apparent in those dark eyes for one infinitesimal second before she turned towards her host.

'Please accept my apologies.'

'Accepted,' drawled Dominic. 'You'll join us in a drink?'

'Chilled water,' Francesca requested with a singularly sweet smile. 'With ice.'

'Bottled? Sparkling or still?'

'Still, if you have it.'

Gabbi hid a faint smile and took another sip of her cocktail.

Francesca had dressed to kill in black, designed perhaps to emphasise her widowed state? She looked every inch the successful international model. The length of her auburn hair was swept into a careless knot, with a few wispy tendrils allowed to escape to frame her face. The make-up was perfection, although Gabbi doubted it had taken Fran more than ten minutes to apply. The perfume was her preferred Hermes Calèche, and there was little doubt that the gown was an Italian designer original bought or bargained for at an outrageously discounted price.

Gabbi wondered how long it would take Dominic to dig beneath Francesca's protective shell and reveal her true nature. Or if Francesca would permit him to try.

Dinner was a convivial meal, the courses varied and many, and while exquisitely presented on the finest bone china they were the antithesis of designer food.

There was, however, an artistically displayed platter of salads adorned with avocado, mango and sprinkled with pine nuts. A subtle concession to what Dominic suspected was a model's necessity to diet? Gabbi wondered.

Francesca, Gabbi knew, ate wisely and well, with little need to watch her intake of food. Tonight, however, she forked dainty portions from each course, declined dessert and opted for herbal tea instead of the ruinously strong black coffee she preferred.

'Northern suburbs, overlooking water and trees in the garden,' Francesca mocked lightly as she met Dominic's level gaze over the rim of her delicate tea-cup.

'Three out of five,' he conceded in a voice that was tinged with humour. 'Are you sufficiently curious to discover if you're right about the remaining two?'

Her eyes were cool. 'The detached studio and a BMW in the garage?'

'Yes.'

One eyebrow lifted. 'A subtle invitation to admire your etchings?'

'I paint in the studio and confine lovemaking to the bedroom.'

Gabbi had to admire Francesca's panache, for there was no artifice in the long, considering look she cast him.

'How—prosaic.'

Give it up, Francesca, Gabbi beseeched silently. You're playing with dynamite. Besides, the 'BMW' is a Lexus and although the studio is detached it's above the treble garage and linked to the house via a glass-enclosed walkway.

'More tea?' Dominic enquired with urbanity.

'Thank you, no.'

Benedict rose to his feet in one smooth movement, his eyes enigmatic as they met those of his wife. 'If you'll excuse us, Dominic?' His smile was warm, and tinged with humour. 'Dinner was superb. Do give our compliments to Louise.'

'It's been a lovely evening,' Gabbi said gently, collecting her purse. She spared Francesca a brief, enquiring glance and could determine little from her friend's expression. Their imminent departure provided an excellent excuse for Francesca to leave, and Gabbi's interest intensified when her friend failed to express that intention.

Perhaps, Gabbi speculated, Francesca was determined not to cut and run at the flimsiest excuse to avoid being alone with Dominic.

'Francesca is quite able to handle herself,' Benedict assured her as he eased the car through the electronically controlled gates and turned onto the street.

'So is Dominic,' Gabbi reminded him as she spared him a frowning glance.

'That worries you?'

'Yes,' she answered starkly. 'I wouldn't like to see Francesca hurt.'

'I failed to see any hint of coercion on Dominic's part,' Benedict returned tolerantly. 'And she chose not to take the opportunity to leave when we did.' He brought the car to a halt at a traffic-controlled intersection.

'Next you'll predict we'll dance at their wedding,' Gabbi declared with a degree of acerbity, and heard his subdued splutter of laughter.

'It wouldn't surprise me.'

'Mario—'

'Is dead,' Benedict stated gently. 'And Francesca is a beautiful young woman who deserves to be happy.'

The lights changed and the car picked up speed. Gabbi turned her attention to the tracery of electric lights on the opposite side of the harbour. It was a picture-postcard scene, and one she'd admired on many occasions in the past. Tonight, however, it failed to hold any attraction.

'You don't think she could fall in love again?'

Gabbi was silent for several long seconds. 'Not the way she loved Mario,' she decided at last.

'Affection, stability and security can be a satisfactory substitute.'

She felt something clench deep inside her, and she caught her breath at the sudden pain. Was that what he thought about *their* marriage? The fire and the passion...were they solely *hers*?

The car traversed the Harbour Bridge, then turned left towards the eastern suburbs. Soon they would be home. And, like the nights that had preceded this one, she would go to sleep in his arms. After the loving.

To deny him was to deny herself. Yet tonight she wanted to, for the sake of sheer perversity.

Gabbi made for the stairs as soon as they entered the house. 'I'll go change.' And slip into the Jacuzzi, she decided as she gained the upper floor. The pulsating jets would ease the tension in her body and help relax her mind.

It didn't, at least not to any satisfactory degree. The doubts that were ever-present in her subconscious rose to the surface with damning ease.

One by one she examined them. Benedict wanted her in his bed, but did he *need* her? *Only* her? Probably not, she admitted sadly, all too aware that there were a hundred women who would rush to take her place. With or without marriage.

One couldn't deny the security factor...for each of them. In her, Benedict had a wife who one day would inherit a share of a billion-dollar corporation, thereby doubling *his* share. Yet, conversely, she also stood to gain.

And stability would be cemented with the addition of children. Why, then, did she continue to take precautions to avoid conception?

Gabbi closed her eyes as images swirled in her mind. The shared joy of early pregnancy, her body swollen with Benedict's child, and afterwards the newborn suckling at her breast.

But it was more than that. Much more. The newborn would develop and grow into a child who became aware of its surroundings, its parents. Financial security would not be an issue. But emotional security?

Divorce had a traumatic effect, and having to accept a stepparent in the place of a loved one was infinitely worse.

Fiercely protective, she wanted desperately for her child to grow up in a happy home with two emotionally committed parents. A marriage based on a business merger lacked the one ingredient essential for a mutually successful long-term relationship: love.

A one-sided love wasn't nearly enough.

Damn. Introspection didn't help at all.

'Sleeping in a Jacuzzi isn't a good idea.'

Gabbi didn't open her eyes. 'I wasn't sleeping.'

'I'm relieved to hear it. Do you intend staying there long?'

'A while.'

He didn't comment, and she sensed rather than heard him leave. Perhaps he'd go downstairs and peruse the latest financial bulletin faxed through from London, New York and Tokyo.

Somehow she doubted he'd simply undress and slide between the sheets, for he was a man who could maintain maximum energy on six hours' sleep in any given twenty-four.

The warm, pulsating water had a soporific effect, and she allowed her thoughts to drift. To her childhood, early treasured memories of her mother, and James. After James followed Monique, and—

Gabbi's eyes flew open as a foot brushed her own. Her startled gaze met a pair of dark brown, almost black eyes heavy with slumberous, vaguely mocking humour.

'What are you doing here?' Why did she sound so—shocked? It was hardly the first time they'd shared the Jacuzzi.

'Is my presence such an unwelcome intrusion?'

'Yes.' Except that wasn't strictly true. 'No,' she amended, unable to tear her eyes away from the strong features within touching distance of her own. Broad cheekbones, a well-defined jaw and the sensual curve of his mouth.

The mouth tilted slightly, and she caught sight of strong white teeth. 'You sound unsure.'

Her gaze didn't waver. 'Perhaps because I am.'

Sinews moved beneath the smooth skin sheathing the powerful breadth of his chest as he extended a hand to trail a gentle pattern across her cheek.

The faint aroma of his cologne had a tantalising

effect on her equilibrium, and her pupils dilated as one finger traced the outline of her lower lip.

Please, she begged silently. Don't do this to me.

Slowly, with infinite patience, he began to erode her defences, breaking them down one by one with the brush of his fingers against the pulse at the base of her throat where it beat in an increasingly visible tattoo.

Those same fingers trailed the contours of each breast, cupped and weighed them in his palm, then teased each tender nub.

Her lips parted and her eyelids drooped low.

No one person should have this much emotional control over another, she thought. There should be some in-built mechanism in one's psyche to prevent such an invasion.

Possession, she substituted as her bones began to liquefy.

Strong hands settled at her waist, and with no effort at all he turned her round to sit in front of him. She felt caged by the strength of his shoulders, the muscled arms that curved beneath her own.

There was warmth, a heat that had nothing to do with the temperature of the water, and when his lips grazed the delicate hollow at the edge of her neck Gabbi sighed in unspoken acceptance.

He had the touch, she mused dreamily, and the knowledge to arouse a woman to the brink of madness. And the control to hold her on the edge until she almost wept for release.

It was a sensual journey that traversed many paths, along which Gabbi had no desire to travel with anyone but him. She knew she'd give up her fortune, her *life*, *everything*…if only he felt the same.

His hands slid to her shoulders, shifting her so that she faced him, and his mouth took possession of her own.

Her arms lifted to encircle his neck, her fingers burying themselves in the thickness of his hair as she held him close.

There was passion as he tasted and took his fill, and she met his raw energy with matching ardour, then let her mouth soften beneath the teasing influence of his, savouring the lingering sweetness, all too aware of the leashed power as he traced the full curve with the tip of his tongue.

She wanted to tease him, test the level of his control. And see if she could break it.

Gabbi let her arms drift down, trailing her fingers over the muscled cord of his neck, taking time to explore the hard ridges, the strong sinews stretching down to each shoulder.

Dark, springy hair covered his chest, and she played with the short curls, twisting them round her fingers, pulling gently, only to release them as she moved to capture a few more.

She lowered her head and touched her lips to his shoulder, then gently trailed a path inch by inch to his ear, using the tip of her tongue with wicked delight on the hollow beneath the lobe before nuzzling and nipping at the sensitive flesh.

With extreme care she caressed the length of his jaw, traced a path across his cheek, then moved to brush each eyelid closed before trailing the slope of his nose.

The sensual mouth was a temptation she couldn't resist, and she touched her lips to its edge, nibbling and tasting as she explored the lower fullness before traversing the upper curve, withdrawing as she felt it firm in preparation to take control.

Gabbi shook her head in silent remonstrance, then slid to her feet and stepped out of the Jacuzzi, grabbed a towel and wrapped it round her slender form, reaching for another as she turned and extended a beckoning hand.

Benedict held her gaze for a few heart-stopping seconds, and she saw his eyes darken with smouldering passion as he reared to his feet.

He loomed large, his frame a testament to male magnificence, muscled sinew moving with easy fluidity, darkened whorls of hair glistening on his water-drenched skin.

His movements were deliberate as he stepped onto the marble-tiled floor, his pace slow as he shortened the distance between them, and his eyes never left hers for a second.

He held out his hand for the towel, and she shook her head, bunching it in her hand as she reached forward to blot the moisture from his skin.

Gabbi began with one shoulder, then the other, and moved to his chest, taking time and care as she slowly traversed his ribcage, his waist, the lean hips, then the muscled length of his powerful thighs. With deliberate casualness she stepped behind him and tended to the width of his back, watching the play of muscles as they flexed and tensed at her touch.

'Nice butt,' she teased gently as she trailed the towel down the back of each thigh.

'You're playing a dangerous game,' Benedict warned with ominous softness as she moved round to stand in front of him.

'Really?' Her lips tilted slightly as she feigned a lack of guile. 'I haven't finished yet.'

'And I haven't even begun.'

Each word possessed the smoothness of silk, and a slight tremor slithered across the surface of her skin.

Was she mad? In setting out to smash his control, was she inviting something she couldn't handle?

Yet she couldn't, *wouldn't* throw in the towel. Literally, she established with a choked laugh as she brushed the thick cotton pile over the matt of dark, curling hair at the apex of his thighs.

A man's arousal was a potent erotic testimony to his sex, his power and his strength. And instrument of a woman's pleasure. With knowledge and expertise, it could drive a woman wild.

Gabbi looked at it with fascination. Unbidden, she trailed the length, gently traced the tip, and brushed a light finger down the shaft.

She wanted to taste him, to use her tongue and her mouth as if she were savouring an exotic confection.

'Do you know what you're inviting?'

Did he read minds? And was it her imagination, or did his voice sound husky and vaguely strained?

She lifted her head and met the burning intensity of his darkened gaze. 'Yes.'

A thrill of anticipatory excitement arrowed through her body at the thought of what demands he might make when caught in the throes of passion. With it came a sense of fear of his strength if it was ever unleashed without restraint.

She swallowed, the only visible sign of her nervousness, and his eyes registered the movement then flicked back to trap her own.

'Then what are you waiting for?' he queried softly. The silent challenge was evident in the depth of his eyes and apparent in the sensual slant of his mouth.

She'd begun this; now she needed to finish it.

Without a word she held out her hand, and felt the enclosing warmth as he clasped it in his own.

In silence Gabbi led him into the bedroom. When she reached the bed she leant forward and dragged the covers free. She turned towards him and placed both hands against his chest, then gently pushed until he lay sprawled against the pale percale sheets.

This was for his pleasure, and she slid down onto her knees beside him.

Slowly she set about exploring every inch of his hair-roughened skin, tangling the tip of her tongue in the whorls and soft curls, the smooth texture that was neither soft nor hard, but wholly male and musky to the taste.

She felt a thrill of satisfaction as muscles tensed and contracted, as she heard the faint catch of his breath, the slight hiss as it was expelled, the soft groan as her hands sought the turgid length of his arousal. With the utmost delicacy she explored the sensitive head, traced the shaft and flicked it gently. Then she lowered her mouth and began a similar exploration with a feather-light touch, allowing sheer instinct to guide her.

Not content, she trailed a path to his hip, traversed the taut stomach, and traced a series of soft kisses to his inner thigh.

With deliberately slow movements she raised her head and looked at him, then she loosened the pins from her hair and shook its length free.

A tiny smile curved her lips as she bent her head and trailed her hair in a teasing path down his chest, past his waist, forming a curtain for the delights her lips offered to the most vulnerable, sensitive part of his anatomy.

Control. He had it. Yet she could only wonder for how long as she lifted her head and lightly traced his moistened shaft with the tips of her fingers.

Her eyes never left his as she brought her fingers up to her mouth, and his eyes flared as she sucked each tip, one by one. Then she rose to her knees and straddled his hips with a graceful movement.

He didn't touch her, but his eyes were dark, so dark they were almost black, and his skin bore the faint flush of restrained passion.

She wanted to kiss him, but didn't dare. This was her game, but there was no doubt who was in charge of the score.

The element of surprise was her only weapon, and she used it shamelessly as she shifted slightly and teased his length with the moist, sensitive heart of her femininity. Then she arched against him, savouring the anticipation of complete possession for a few heart-stopping seconds before she accepted him in a long, slow descent.

Totally enclosed, she felt him swell even further, and gasped at the sensation. Then she began to move, enjoying the feeling of partial loss followed by complete enclosure in a slow, circling dance that tore at the level of her own control.

Her fingers tightened their grip on his shoulders as she fought against the insidious demands of desire, and she cried out when his hands caught hold of her hips and held them, steadying her as he thrust deep inside her, then repeated the action again and again until she became lost to the rhythm, mindless, in a vortex of emotion.

When she was spent he slid a hand behind her nape and brought her head down to rest against him.

Gabbi lay still, her breathing gradually slowing in tune with his. There was a sense of power, of satisfaction that had little to do with sexual climax in her post-orgasmic state. His skin was warm and damp and tasted vaguely of salt. She savoured it, and felt the spasm of hard-muscled flesh within her own.

Did a man experience this sensation of glory after taking a woman? That the sexual symphony he'd orchestrated and conducted had climaxed with such a wondrous crescendo?

And when it was over, did he want an encore?

Gabbi lifted her head and stared down at the slumberous warmth in Benedict's dark eyes, glimpsed the latent humour in their depths and caught the soft slant of his mouth.

'Thank you,' he murmured gently as he angled her

mouth down to meet his in a possession that was a simulation of what they'd just shared.

His hand slid down her spine, and she gasped as he rolled with her until she felt the mattress beneath her back.

It was a long while before she lay curled in the circle of his arms. As an encore, it had surpassed all that had gone before. And, she reflected a trifle sadly, it was she who had lost control, she who had cried out in the throes of passion.

On the edge of sleep, she told herself she didn't care. If pleasure was the prize, it was possible to win even when you lost.

CHAPTER SIX

WHY was it that some days were destined to be more eventful than others? Gabbi wondered silently as she entered the house and made her way through to the kitchen.

She'd been very calm at the board meeting when Maxwell Fremont had verbally challenged her to explain in minute detail why it would be beneficial to re-finance a subsidiary arm to maximise the company's tax advantage. The initial margin was narrow, given the re-financing costs involved, but the long-term prospect was considerably more favourable than the existing financial structure. Her research had been thorough, the figure projections carefully checked, and there had been a degree of satisfaction when the proposal had gained acceptance.

The afternoon had concluded with a misplaced file and a computer glitch, and on the way home a careless motorist hadn't braked in time and her car had suffered a few scratches and a broken tail-light. Which was a nuisance, for insurance red tape meant that the Mercedes would be out of action while the damage was assessed, and again when it went into the workshop for repair.

A few laps of the swimming pool, followed by an alfresco meal on the terrace, held more appeal than dressing up and attending a formal fund-raising ball.

However, the ball was a prominent annual event for which Benedict had tickets and a vague disinclination to attend was not sufficient reason to initiate a protest. Although the thought of crossing verbal swords with Annaliese over pâté, roast beef and chocolate mousse wasn't Gabbi's idea of a fun evening.

And any minute now Benedict would drive into the garage, see a smashed tail-light and demand an explanation.

She crossed to the refrigerator, filled a glass with fresh orange juice and took a long, appreciative swallow.

'Care to tell me what happened?'

Right on cue. She looked at him and rolled her eyes. 'Heavy traffic, a driver more intent on his mobile phone conversation than the road, the lights changed, I stopped, he didn't.' That about encapsulated it. 'We exchanged names and insurance details,' she concluded.

He crossed to where she stood and his fingers probed the back of her neck. 'Headache? Any symptoms of whiplash?'

'No.' His concern was gratifying, but his standing this close didn't do much to stabilise her equilibrium. 'Traffic was crawling at the time.'

'Want to cancel out on tonight?'

She looked at him carefully. 'What if I said yes?'

'I'd make a phone call and we'd stay at home.'

'Just like that?' One eyebrow rose. 'I didn't realise I held such power. Aren't you worried I might misuse it?'

His hand slid forward and captured her chin, tilting

AN IMPORTANT MESSAGE FROM THE EDITORS OF HARLEQUIN®

Dear Reader,

Because you've chosen to read one of our fine romance novels, we'd like to say "thank you"! And, as a **special** way to thank you, we've selected <u>four more</u> of the <u>books</u> you love so well, **and** a beautiful Cherub Magnet to send you absolutely *FREE!*

Please enjoy them with our compliments...

Candy Lee

Editor,
Presents

P.S. And because we value our customers, we've attached something extra inside ...

EDITOR'S
FREE GIFT SEAL
THANK YOU

PEEL OFF SEAL AND PLACE INSIDE

HOW TO VALIDATE
YOUR
EDITOR'S FREE GIFT
"THANK YOU"

1. Peel off gift seal from front cover. Place it in space provided at right. This automatically entitles you to receive four free books and a lovely Cherub Magnet.

2. Send back this card and you'll get brand-new Harlequin Presents® novels. These books have a cover price of $3.50 each, but they are yours to keep absolutely free.

3. There's no catch. You're under no obligation to buy anything. We charge nothing — ZERO — for your first shipment. And you don't have to make any minimum number of purchases — not even one!

4. The fact is thousands of readers enjoy receiving books by mail from the Harlequin Reader Service® . They like the convenience of home delivery...they like getting the best new novels BEFORE they're available in stores...and they love our discount prices!

5. We hope that after receiving your free books you'll want to remain a subscriber. But the choice is yours — to continue or cancel, anytime at all! So why not take us up on our invitation, with no risk of any kind. You'll be glad you did!

6. Don't forget to detach your FREE BOOKMARK. And remember...just for validating your Editor's Free Gift Offer, we'll send you FIVE MORE gifts, *ABSOLUTELY FREE!*

This charming refrigerator magnet looks like a little cherub, and it's a perfect size for holding notes and recipes. Best of all it's yours ABSOLUTELY FREE when you accept our NO-RISK offer!

it slightly so that he could examine her expression. 'Not your style, Gabbi.'

At this precise moment she felt disinclined to pursue an in-depth evaluation. 'What time do you want to leave?'

He released her and crossed to the refrigerator. 'Seven.'

She had an hour, part of which she intended to spend indulging in a leisurely shower.

In the bedroom she stripped down to her underwear then crossed to the bathroom and activated the water.

Bliss, she acknowledged several minutes later as she rinsed off shampoo and allowed the water to stream down her back. Scented soap freshened her skin with a delicate fragrance, and she lifted her hands to slick back her hair.

The glass door slid open and Benedict stepped into the stall. His naked body ignited a familiar fire deep inside her, and she attempted to dampen it down. 'I've almost finished.' How could her voice sound so calm, so matter-of-fact, when inside she was slowly going up in flames? she wondered.

Would he...? No, there wasn't time. Unless they were to arrive late...

Gabbi subconsciously held her breath as he moved behind her, then released it as his hands settled on her shoulders. Firm fingers began a soothing massage that felt good. So good that she murmured her appreciation.

She let her head fall forward as he worked the tense muscles and she relaxed, unwilling to move.

'Fremont gave you a hard time at the board meeting this morning.'

'Anticipating his queries kept me on my toes.'

'You came well prepared.'

'Being *family* isn't regarded by some as an advantage,' she responded dryly.

'Should it be?'

'You obviously didn't think so.'

Benedict's fingers didn't still. 'My father was a very powerful man. I chose not to compete on his turf.'

'Yet you're where he wanted you to be.'

'There was never any question I wouldn't eventually take his place.'

No, just a matter of when, Gabbi added silently, and wondered whether destiny had played a part. For if Conrad hadn't died Benedict would still be living in America. And the marriage between Benedict Nicols and Gabbi Stanton would not have taken place. It was a sobering thought.

She lifted her head and moved away from him. 'I must get ready.' He made no attempt to stop her as she stepped out of the stall.

It took fifteen minutes to dry and style her hair, a further fifteen to complete her make-up. The gown she'd chosen to wear was dramatic black in a figure-hugging design with shoestring shoulder-straps. Long black gloves added glamour, as did jewellery, black hosiery and stiletto-heeled evening shoes. A few dabs of her favourite perfume completed the image.

Benedict's frame, height and looks were guaranteed to weaken a woman's knees no matter what he wore...or didn't wear. In a tailored black evening suit and white cotton shirt he was positively awesome.

Gabbi cast him a studied glance, and felt the familiar trip of her pulse as it leapt to a quickened beat. The heat flared inside her stomach and slowly spread, licking each nerve-ending into vibrant life.

Less than an hour ago she'd stood naked with him in the shower, yet she felt more acutely vulnerable *now*, fully clothed, than she had then.

To dispel the feeling she spread her arms, completed a full turn and summoned a mischievous smile. 'What do you think?'

His eyes were dark, and his mouth tugged wide over gleaming teeth as he deliberated.

Perhaps she should have worn her hair down, instead of caught into a carelessly contrived knot? Was black too dramatic, too stark?

'Stunning,' Benedict complimented, and saw relief beneath her carefully guarded expression.

'Flattery is an excellent way to begin the evening,' Gabbi said lightly as she turned away to collect her evening bag.

Thirty minutes later a parking valet swept the Bentley down into the vast concrete cavern beneath the hotel as she walked at Benedict's side through the main entrance.

Smile-time, show-time. She knew she shouldn't be such a cynic at twenty-five. Yet *years* spent taking an active part in the social scene had taught her she was expected to play a part. And she'd learned to do it well—the radiant smile, the light-hearted greeting, the spontaneous small talk.

The Grand Ballroom looked resplendent with its decorative theme, the DJ had unobtrusive mood-music playing, and impeccably uniformed waiters and waitresses hovered dutifully, taking and delivering drink orders.

A sell-out, one of the committee members delighted in informing Benedict as she directed him to their appointed table.

Gabbi entertained the slight hope that Annaliese might bring a partner, and she brightened visibly for all of two seconds before recognising the man on her stepsister's arm as none other than Dominic Andrea. More of a mismatch was difficult to imagine, and hot on the heels of that thought was...*what about Francesca*?

'A migraine,' Dominic said for her ears only as he seated Annaliese on his right and then slid into the seat beside Gabbi. 'Annaliese's date will be late.'

A smile curved her mouth. 'You read minds?'

'I anticipated your reaction.'

'Am I that transparent?'

His smile was slow and his eyes sparkled with devilish humour.

'Subtlety isn't my strong point.'

No, but determination was. She thought of Francesca and smiled. If Dominic was intent on pursuit, Francesca didn't have much of a chance.

'She intrigues me.'

Gabbi's smile widened. 'I had noticed.'

'Wish me luck?'

'All you need.'

James arrived with Monique and they took the seats

opposite, exchanged greetings, and placed orders with
the drinks waiter.

Monique looked radiant in a royal blue gown and
a matching evening jacket. Sapphire and diamond
jewellery graced her neck and her wrist, and a large
sapphire and diamond dress ring on her right hand
almost eclipsed the magnificent diamond above her
wedding band.

Annaliese had chosen deep emerald silk that
hugged her curves like a second skin, with a side-split
that bordered on the indecent.

The two remaining couples at their table slid into
their seats as the DJ changed CDs and played an introductory number that was followed by the charity
chairman's welcoming speech.

A prawn cocktail starter was served. Soft music filtered unobtrusively while the guests ate, providing a
pleasant background.

The main course followed, comprising grilled
chicken breast served with mango sauce and vegetables.

Delicious, Gabbi complimented silently as she
forked delicate portions. A sandwich eaten at her desk
around midday seemed inadequate sustenance by
comparison.

A few sips of excellent Chardonnay proved relaxing, and she listened with interest as the host extolled
the virtues of the charity, cited the money raised at
this evening's event and thanked various sponsors for
their generous donations.

A tall male figure slid into the empty seat beside

Annaliese and, when the speech was concluded, Annaliese performed the necessary introductions.

Not that one was needed. Aaron Jacob was equally well-known as an eminently successful male model as he was as a star in a long-running television series.

A heartthrob and a hunk, Gabbi acknowledged in feminine appreciation of a near-perfect male specimen. Pity he had an inflated ego and a reputation for changing his dates as often as his socks!

As a couple, Annaliese and Aaron were guaranteed to have their photo prominently displayed on the society page in tomorrow's newspaper. Perhaps that was the purpose of their date? *Be nice,* Gabbi silently chided in self-admonishment as she sipped her wine.

Soon the DJ would increase the volume of the music and invite guests to take to the dance floor. It would be a signal for everyone to mix and mingle, dance and provide an opportunity for the society doyennes to flaunt their latest designer gowns.

'More wine?'

Gabbi turned slightly and met Benedict's warm gaze. 'No, thanks. I'd prefer water.'

One eyebrow lifted in silent enquiry, and she offered him a brilliant smile. 'I thought you might like me to drive home.'

'Considerate of you.' His quiet drawl held a degree of musing cynicism, aware as she was that he rarely took more than one glass of wine with an evening meal and that therefore the offer was unnecessary.

'Yes, isn't it?'

'Benedict.'

Monique's intrusion commanded his attention.

'I've managed to get a few tickets to *Phantom of the Opera*, Wednesday evening. You and Gabrielle will join us, won't you?'

Was it coincidence that Monique had tickets for the same night that Gabbi and Benedict had invited Francesca and Dominic to make up a foursome?

'Thank you, Monique. I already have tickets.'

'Perhaps we could arrange to meet afterwards for supper?'

Familial togetherness was a fine thing, Gabbi acknowledged. But Monique's stage-managing was becoming a little overt.

'Unfortunately we've made other arrangements.'

'Annaliese and Gabrielle are so close, and see so little of each other.' Monique injected just the right amount of regret into her voice then moved in for the figurative kill. 'It seems such a shame not to take advantage of every opportunity to get together while Annaliese is home.'

Oh, my, her stepmother was good. Gabbi almost held her breath, waiting for Benedict's response.

'Another time, Monique.'

'You must come to dinner. Just family. Monday, Tuesday? Either evening is free.'

Persistence, thy name is Monique!

'Gabbi?'

That's right, she thought wryly; pass the buck. Avoiding the dinner was impossible, therefore decisiveness was the only way to go. 'Monday. We'll look forward to it.' Were polite lies considered *real* lies? If so, she'd be damned in hell. Yet she felt justified in telling them for her father's sake.

'Shall we dance?'

Now there was a question. Dancing with Benedict inevitably became a dangerous pleasure. 'Thank you, darling.' She rose to her feet and allowed him to lead her onto the dance floor.

The Celine Dion number was perfect, the lyrics revealing a certain poignancy that echoed most women's hopes and dreams.

Gabbi's body fitted the contours of his with easy familiarity, and she had the crazy desire to discard her conventional hold and wind her arms round his neck.

Did he sense how she felt? He was the very air that she breathed. Everything she wanted, all she would ever need. In a way it was frightening. What if she ever lost him?

'Cold?'

She lifted her head and looked at him for a few seconds without comprehension.

'You shivered,' Benedict enlightened her gently.

Get a grip, Gabbi, she chided herself. She summoned a smile and dismissed it lightly. 'Old ghosts.'

'Want to go back to the table?'

'You think I need to conserve my strength?' she queried solemnly as he led her to the edge of the dance floor.

'Tomorrow's Saturday.'

She shot him a sparkling smile. 'An hour of morning decadence before enjoying a late breakfast on the terrace?'

'*Early*-morning decadence, breakfast on the terrace, followed by a drive to the airport.'

'We're *escaping*?' Gabbi looked at him with due

reverence. 'Alone? *Where?* No, don't tell me. Someone might overhear.'

'Witch,' he murmured close to her ear.

Dessert was served as they resumed their seats, followed by coffee and after-dinner mints.

Annaliese drifted onto the dance floor with Aaron,
then paused and posed for a vigilant photographer.

'May I?'

Gabbi glanced at Dominic and rose to her feet.
Benedict broke his conversation with James and cast
her a quick smile.

'Benedict is selective with men who want to partner
his wife.'

Gabbi cast Dominic a startled glance as he led her
towards the dance floor and pulled her gently into his
arms.

'Don't you believe me?'

How did she respond to that? Her light, amused
laugh seemed relatively noncommittal.

They circled the floor, twice, then Dominic stepped
to one side as Aaron and Annaliese suggested an
exchange in partners.

Gabbi smiled as she moved into Aaron's clasp, then
winced as he pulled her close. Too close.

'Watch my show?' The query was smooth, and she
felt reluctant to enter the game he expected every female to play.

'No, I don't.' She tried to sound vaguely regretful,
but it didn't quite come off.

'You don't watch television?'

The temptation to take him down was difficult to
resist. 'Of course. Mainly news and documentaries.'

'You're a brain.'

Gabbi wasn't sure it was a compliment. 'We all have one.'

'In my business you have to look after the body. It's the visual thing, you know? Nutrition, gym, beauty therapist, manicurist, hair stylist. Waxing's the worst.'

'Painful,' she agreed.

'Oh, yeah,' he conceded with a realistic shudder. 'I'm jetting out to LA next week. Been offered a part in a film. Could be the big break.'

She attempted enthusiasm. 'Good luck.'

'Thanks.'

'Mind if I cut in?'

Gabbi heard the quiet, drawling tone and detected the faint edge to her husband's voice.

'Sure.' Aaron relinquished her without argument.

'You interrupted an interesting conversation,' she said mildly as Benedict drew her close.

'Define interesting.'

'Waxing body hair. His.'

'Up front and personal, hmm?'

She stifled a bubble of laughter. 'Oh, yeah,' she agreed in wicked imitation.

As they circled the floor she wondered how he would react if she said she hungered to feel his skin next to her own, his mouth in possession of hers in the slow dance towards sexual fulfilment.

'Darling Gabrielle. Isn't it about time I danced with my brother-in-law?'

No. And he isn't. At least, not technically. However, the words stayed locked in her throat as she graciously acknowledged Annaliese and moved into Dominic's arms.

'I was outfoxed,' Dominic murmured, and Gabbi offered a philosophical smile. 'Want me to complete a round of the floor, intervene and switch partners?'

'No, but thanks anyway.'

A few minutes later there was a break in the music and they returned to the table.

Gabbi collected her evening bag and with a murmured excuse she moved towards the foyer with the intention of freshening her make-up in an adjacent powder room.

There was a queue, and it was some time before she was able to find free space at the mirror to effect repairs.

A number of people had escaped the ballroom to smoke in the adjoining foyer, and Gabbi exchanged a greeting with one guest, then another, before turning to re-enter the ballroom.

'Ah, there you are, darling.' Annaliese projected a high-voltage smile. 'I was sent on a rescue mission.'

'By whom?'

Annaliese's eyes widened in artful surprise. 'Why, Benedict. Who else?'

'An absence of ten minutes hardly constitutes the need for a search party,' Gabbi said evenly.

Annaliese examined the perfection of her manicured nails.

'Benedict likes to guard his possessions.'

Attack was the best form of defence, yet Gabbi opted for a tactical sidestep. 'Yes.'

'Doesn't it bother you?'

'What, precisely?'

'Being regarded as an expensive ornament in a wealthy man's collection.'

This could get nasty without any effort at all. 'A trophy wife?' Gabbi arched one eyebrow and proffered a winsome smile. 'Did it ever occur to you to examine the reverse situation? In Benedict I have an attentive husband who indulges my slightest whim.' She ticked off the advantages one by one. 'He's attractive, socially eminent and he's good in bed.' She allowed the smile to widen. 'I consider I made the perfect choice.'

A flash of fury was clearly evident before Annaliese managed to conquer it. 'You seem a little peaky, darling. Pre-menstrual tension?'

'Sibling aggravation,' Gabbi corrected her, resisting the temptation to add more fuel to her stepsister's fire. 'Shall we return to the ballroom?'

'I intend to use the powder room.'

'In that case...' She paused, and effected a faint lift of her shoulder. 'See you back at the table.'

The minor victory was sweet, but she entertained no doubt that the war was far from over. However, a weekend away would provide a welcome break from the battlefield. The thought was enough to lighten her expression and bring a smile to her lips.

Benedict was deep in conversation with Dominic, Aaron and Monique were conducting animated small talk and James seemed content being an observer. Gabbi took the vacant seat beside her father.

'Would you like some more coffee?'

She shook her head. 'You could ask me to dance.'

A smile slanted his mouth. 'Dear, sweet Gabbi. I'm honoured.' He rose to his feet and held out his hand. 'Shall we?'

'Enjoying yourself?'

Gabbi considered his question as they circled the dance floor, and opted to counter it. 'Are you?'

'Monique assures me such occasions are a social advantage.'

'I suspect she considers you need a welcome break from wheeling and dealing,' she teased lightly, and incurred his soft laughter.

'More likely a woman's ploy to justify spending a small fortune on a new gown and half the day being pampered by a beautician and hairdresser.'

'Which men are content to allow, in the knowledge that said social occasions provide equal opportunity for proposing or cementing a business deal.'

He spared her a thoughtful glance. 'Do I detect a note of cynicism?'

'Perhaps.'

'Benedict adores you.'

She could accept respect and affection, but wasn't *adore* a little over the top? Fortunately with James there was no need to perpetuate the myth. 'He's very good to me.'

'I would never have sanctioned the marriage if I hadn't been convinced that he would take care of you.'

The music wound down for a break between numbers, and Gabbi preceded her father to their table.

Annaliese had taken an empty seat next to Benedict, Monique was conversing with Dominic and

Aaron was nowhere in sight. Musical chairs, Gabbi decided with a touch of black humour as she slid into a vacant one.

Guests were slowly beginning to dissipate. In half an hour the bar would close and the DJ would shut down for the night. Any time soon they could begin drifting towards the foyer, take the lift to the main entrance and have the doorman summon their car.

Benedict lifted his head at that moment and cast her a searching glance, raised one eyebrow a fraction, then smoothly extricated himself from Annaliese's clutches. Literally, as the scarlet-tipped fingers of one hand trailed a persuasive path down the fabric sheathing his forearm, followed by a coy smile and an upward sweep of mascaraed eyelashes in a deliberate attempt at flirtation.

Gabbi tried to assure herself that it didn't matter. But it did.

She smiled graciously all the way to the main entrance, completed the air-kiss routine with Monique and Annaliese, brushed lips over her father's cheek, bade Dominic and Aaron goodnight, then slipped into the passenger seat of the Bentley.

Benedict eased the car towards the busy main street, paused until he gained clear passage into the flow of traffic then quickly increased speed.

Gabbi leaned her head back and focused her attention on the view of the city. Bright flashing neon signs and illuminated shop windows soon gave way to inner-city suburban streets and shuttered windows, some dark, others showing a glimmer of muted electricity. And, as they began to ascend the New South

Head road, they gained a view of the harbour, its waters darkened by night and tipped with ribbons of reflected light.

'You're very quiet.'

She turned her head and examined Benedict's shadowed profile. 'I was enjoying the peaceful silence after several hours of music and noisy chatter.' It was true, but she doubted he was fooled by her explanation. 'If there's something you want to discuss…' She trailed off, and gave a slight shrug.

'Annaliese.'

No doubt about it, he aimed straight for the main target. But two could play at that game.

The Bentley turned into their street, slowed as they reached the electronically controlled gates guarding their property, swept along the curved driveway and came to a halt inside the garage.

Gabbi released the seat belt, unfastened the door-clasp and slid out of the car, aware that Benedict was mirroring her actions. He attended to the house alarm and followed her indoors, keyed in the re-set code then drew her into the lounge.

'Would you like a drink?'

She looked at him carefully, and chose a light-hearted response. 'Champagne.'

He crossed to the bar, removed a bottle from the fridge, opened it, filled two flutes then retraced his steps.

Gabbi took one flute and raised it in a silent salute, then sipped the contents. 'What particular aspect of my stepsister's character do you want to discuss?'

She could read nothing in his expression, and she

had no idea whether he intended to damn her with faint praise or offer a compliment on her remarkable restraint.

'Annaliese's determination to cause trouble.'

Gabbi allowed her eyes to widen measurably, and she placed a hand over her heart. 'Oh, my goodness. I hadn't noticed.'

'Don't be facetious.'

'It's *obvious*?'

'Stop it, Gabbi,' Benedict warned.

'Why? I'm on a roll.'

'Quit while you're ahead.'

'OK. Pick a scenario. Annaliese wants you, you want her. Annaliese wants you, you don't want her.'

'The latter.'

She hadn't realised she'd been holding her breath, and she released it slowly. 'Well, now, that's a relief. I can kiss goodbye visions of throwing out monogrammed towels, ruining your hand-stitched shoes and cutting up every one of your suits.' She gave him a hard smile that didn't quite match the vulnerability apparent in her eyes. 'I had intentions of being quite vicious if you decided on divorce.'

Humour gleamed in those dark eyes, and a deep chuckle emerged from his throat.

'It's not funny.'

'No.'

'Then don't laugh. I was serious.'

Benedict took a long swallow of champagne and placed his flute down on a nearby pedestal. 'Why in hell would I consider divorcing a sassy young woman who delights in challenging me on every level in favour of someone like Annaliese?' He removed her champagne flute and lowered it to join his own. Then he pulled her into his arms.

Gabbi didn't have a chance to answer before his mouth closed over hers, and she drank in the taste of him mingled with the sweet tang of vintage French champagne, generously giving everything he asked, more than he demanded, until mutual need spiralled to the edge of their control.

'I could take you here, now,' Benedict groaned huskily as his lips grazed a path down her throat, and she arched her head to allow him easy access to the sensitive hollow at its base, the swell of her breasts as he trailed lower.

A soft laugh choked in her throat as he freed one tender globe and took a liberty with its peak. Then she cried out as he lifted her over one shoulder and began striding from the room.

'Caveman tactics,' she accused as he ascended the stairs.

He gained the upper floor, then headed for the main suite. When he reached it, he released her to stand within the circle of his arms.

'Want to undress me?'

Her eyes sparkled with wicked humour. 'Might be quicker if you did it yourself.'

'That bad, huh?'

'Yes,' she said with honest simplicity, her own fingers as busy as his as clothes layered the carpet.

Their loving was all heat and hunger the first time round, followed by a long, sweet after-play that led to the slow slaking of mutual need.

Afterwards she lay with her head pillowed against his chest, the sound of his heartbeat beneath her cheek.

'I don't think I could bear to lose you,' Gabbi said, on the edge of sleep, and wasn't sure whether she heard or dreamed his response.

'What makes you think you will?'

CHAPTER SEVEN

QUEENSLAND'S Gold Coast lay little more than an hour's flight north of Sydney, and the Stanton-Nicols' Lear jet ensured private airport access, luxurious cabin space and personalised service.

Cleared for take-off, the streamlined jet cruised the runway and achieved a rapid ascent before levelling out.

'No laptop?' Gabbi quizzed as she loosened her seat belt. 'No papers in your briefcase?'

Benedict sank back in his chair and regarded her with indolent amusement. 'Each within easy access.'

'Are you going to work during the flight?'

'Would you prefer me to?'

'No.' Her eyes assumed a mischievous gleam. 'It's not often I get one hour of your undivided attention.' She saw one eyebrow slant, and quickly qualified this. 'Alone. Out of the bedroom,' she added, then spread her hands in helpless acceptance at having stepped into a verbal quagmire. 'I'll give up while I'm ahead.'

'Wise.'

'Coffee, Mr Nicols? Juice, Mrs Nicols?'

'Thanks, Melanie.'

The cabin stewardess's intrusion was timely. Her smile was professional as she unloaded the tray, then poured coffee and juice. 'I'll be in the cockpit. Buzz me if you need anything.'

Gabbi leaned forward, picked up the glass of fresh orange juice and took an appreciative sip. 'Tell me about the deal you and James are involved in with Gibson Electronics.'

He proceeded to do so, answering her queries as she debated various points.

'It's tight, but fair,' she conceded after a lengthy discussion. 'Think we'll pull it off?'

'Gibson needs Stanton-Nicols' proven reputation with the Asian market.'

'And in return we gain a slice of Gibson Electronics.'

Business. The common factor that forged the link between them. Without it, she doubted she'd be Benedict Nicols' wife. A chilling thought, and one she chose not to dwell on.

The 'fasten seat belt' sign flashed on as the jet began its descent towards Coolangatta airport.

A car was waiting for them, and it took only a few minutes to transfer the minimal luggage into the boot. Benedict signalled to the pilot and had a brief word with the driver while Gabbi took the passenger seat, then he strode round and slid in behind the wheel.

The Gold Coast was Australia's major tourist mecca. Long, sweeping beaches, surf, golden sands, towering high-rise buildings, modern shopping complexes and a subtropical climate all combined to make it a highly sought-after holiday destination. Theme parks, a casino, hotels, cruise boats, canal developments and luxurious prestige housing estates promoted a lifestyle that belonged in part to the rich and famous.

Gabbi loved the casual atmosphere, the spacious residential sprawl. A city with few disadvantages, she mused as Benedict joined the north-bound traffic.

High-rise apartment buildings lined the foreshore, their names varying from the prosaic to the exotic. Warm temperatures, sunshine, azure-blue sky, palm fronds swaying beneath a gentle breeze.

A smile curved her generous mouth, and her eyes filled with latent laughter. Paradise. And Benedict. They were hers for two days.

Conrad and Diandra Nicols had purchased a beach-front block of land and built a three-level vacation home in the days before prestigious real estate lining Mermaid Beach's Hedges Avenue had gained multi-million-dollar price-tags.

Benedict had chosen to retain it as an investment, persuaded from time to time to lease it short-term to visiting dignitaries who desired the privacy of a personal residence instead of a hotel suite or apartment block. Gabbi loved its location, its direct access onto the beach and the open-plan design.

A sigh of pure pleasure left her lips as Benedict drew the car to a halt before the electronically controlled gates, depressed the modem that released them and keyed in a code to operate the garage doors.

The three-car garage was backed by a games-room that led out to a terraced swimming pool. The first level comprised an office, lounge, kitchen and dining-room, with a master suite, three guest bedrooms and two bathrooms on the upper floor.

Each level was connected by a wide curved staircase leading onto a semi-circular, balustraded landing, providing a circular central space highlighted by a magnificent chandelier suspended from the top-level ceiling and reaching down to almost touching distance from the ground-level entertainment room. Lit up at night, it was a spectacular sight.

'You sound like a student let out of school,' Benedict commented as they ascended the stairs to the uppermost floor.

'I love it here,' she said simply as she swung round to face¯him.

'What do you suggest we do with the day?'

'Oh, my, what a responsibility.' Her eyes danced with impish humour, and she pretended to deliberate. 'I could drag you off to visit a theme park. We could hire a boat and cruise the broadwater. Do a bit of sun-worshipping by the pool. Or take in a movie at the cinema.' Her mouth curved into a winsome smile. 'On the other hand, I could be an understanding wife and tell you to go set up a game of golf... something you'd enjoy.'

Benedict reached out a hand and brushed light fingers across her cheek. 'And in return?'

'I get to choose where we have dinner.'

'Done.' He bent down and gave her a brief, hard kiss. 'We'll go on to a show or the movies.'

'You ring the golf course while I unpack.' She had a plan, and she put it into action. 'Do you want to take the four-wheel drive or the sedan?'

'The four-wheel drive.'

Half an hour later she backed the sedan out of the garage and headed for the nearest major shopping complex. It was fun to browse the boutiques, sip a cappuccino, before getting down to the serious business of shopping.

She had a list, and she entered the food hall, selected a trolley and began.

It was almost midday when she re-entered the house with no less than five carrier bags, the contents of which were systematically stored in the refrigerator and pantry.

The menu was basic. The accompanying sauces would be anything but. Wine, French breadsticks. A delicious tiramisu for dessert. Liqueur coffee. And she had hired a video.

At five she set the table with fine linen and lace, silver cutlery and china. Then she checked the kitchen and went upstairs to shower. After selecting fresh underwear, she donned elegant blue silk evening trousers and a matching top, then groomed her hair into a smooth knot on top of her head. She then tended to her make-up, which was understated, with just a hint of blusher, soft eyeshadow and a touch of clear rose-pink lip-gloss.

It was after six when the security system beeped, alerting her to the fact that the gates were being released, followed by the garage doors. She heard a refined clunk as the vehicle door closed, then Benedict came into view.

Gabbi stilled the nervous fluttering inside her stomach as she moved out onto the landing to greet him.

He looked magnificent. Dark hair teased by a faint breeze. Broad shoulders and superb musculature emphasised by a navy open-necked polo shirt. Strong facial features, tanned a deeper shade by several hours spent in the sun.

'Hi. How was the game?'

He looked intensely male, emanating a slight air of aggressive goodwill that spoke of achievement and satisfaction at having pitted his skill against a rival and won.

He reached the landing and moved towards her, pausing to bestow a brief, evocative kiss. 'I'll hit the shower.'

'Don't bother dressing.'

One eyebrow lifted and his lips twisted to form a humorous smile. 'My dear Gabbi. You want me to be arrested?'

'We're eating in.' Now that she'd taken the decision upon herself, she was unsure of his reaction. 'I've made dinner.'

He looked at her carefully, noting the slight uncertainty, the faint nervousness apparent, and her effort to camouflage it. 'Give me ten minutes.'

He rejoined her in nine. Freshly shaven, showered, and dressed in casual trousers and a short-sleeved shirt.

'Would you like a drink?'

Gabbi shook her head. 'You have one. I'll wait until we eat.'

He followed her into the kitchen, caught sight of numerous saucepans washed and stacked to drain. 'Looks professional. Smells delicious. Hidden talents, Gabbi?'

She wrinkled her nose at him, then swatted his hand as he reached forward to sample the sauce. 'No advance tasting, no peeking. Open the wine. It needs to breathe.'

She served the starter. Delicate stuffed mushrooms that melted in the mouth. French bread heated to crunchy perfection.

The main course was an exquisite *filet mignon* so tender that the flesh parted at the slightest pressure of the knife. With it they had asparagus with hollandaise sauce, baby potatoes in their jackets split and anointed with garlic butter and glazed baby carrots.

When they'd finished, Benedict touched his glass to hers in a silent salute. 'I haven't tasted better in any restaurant.'

'To the French, food is a passion. The meals I shared with Jacques's family were gastronomical feasts, visual works of art.' Her eyes sparkled with remembered pleasure. 'I made a deal with his mother,' she said solemnly.

'You kept your hands off her son, and she taught you to cook?'

Gabbi began to laugh. 'Close.'

'One look at you and any mother would fear for her son's emotional sanity,' Benedict drawled.

She met his gaze and held it. What about *his* emotional sanity? Was it so controlled that no woman could disturb it?

'I'll get dessert.' She rose to her feet and stacked his plate and cutlery with her own, then took them through to the kitchen.

Two wide individual crystal bowls held the creamy ambrosia of liqueur-soaked sponge, cream and shaved chocolate that was tiramisu.

It was good; she'd even have said delicious.

Benedict sat back in his chair and discarded his napkin. 'Superb, Gabbi.'

She lifted one shoulder in a negligible shrug. 'We dine out so often, I thought it would make a change to stay home.'

'I'll help with the dishes.'

'All done,' she assured lightly. 'I'll make coffee. There's a video in the VCR.'

When the coffee had filtered, she poured it, added liqueur and topped it with cream, then took both stemmed glasses through to the lounge.

Benedict had chosen one of three double-seater leather settees, and he indicated the empty space beside him.

The movie was a comedy, loosely adapted from the original *La cage aux folies*. It was amusing, well acted and entertaining.

Gabbi sipped her coffee slowly, then, when she had finished, Benedict took the glass and placed it together with his on a side table.

She relaxed and leaned her head back against the cushioned rest. Being here like this was magical. No guests, no intrusions.

An arm curved round her shoulders and drew her close. She felt his breath stir her hair. And she made no protest as he used a modem to switch off the lights.

The only illumination came from the television screen, and the electric candles reflected from the chandelier. Which he dimmed.

Awareness flared as his fingers brushed against her breast and stayed. His lips lingered at her temple.

She let her hand rest on his thigh, and didn't explore.

Occasionally his fingers would move in an absent pattern that quickened her pulse and triggered the heat deep inside her.

It was a delightful, leisurely prelude to a rhapsody that would gather momentum and crest in a passionate climax.

Gabbi wasn't disappointed. Just when she thought there were no more paths she could travel, Benedict took her along another, gently coaxing, pacing his pleasure to match her own before tipping her over the edge.

Close to sleep, she whispered, *Je t'aime, mon amour,* to the measured heartbeat beneath her lips. And wondered if he heard, if he knew.

They rose early and took a leisurely walk along the beach, then stripped down to swimwear and ventured into the ocean.

The water was cool and calm, the waves tame, and afterwards they sprinted back to the house and rinsed the sea from their skin and hair, donned casual clothes and ate a hearty breakfast out on the terrace.

'How do you feel about a drive to the mountains?'

Gabbi took a sip of coffee, then rested the cup between both hands. Visions of a picnic lunch and panoramic views were enticing. 'What of the call you're expecting?'

Benedict subjected her to a measured appraisal, then moved his shoulders in an indolent gesture. 'Divert the house phone to my mobile, sling the briefcase and laptop onto the rear seat.'

It wasn't often he took an entire weekend off. All too frequently his time was spent in the study in front of the computer, surfing various global financial sites on the Internet. Leisure was relegated to social occasions, and even then business was inevitably an ongoing topic of discussion.

Hesitation wasn't an option. 'Let's do it.' She replaced her cup on the table and rose to her feet. 'I'll make sandwiches.'

He put a restraining hand on her arm. 'We'll pick up something along the way.'

The phone rang, and Gabbi froze as Benedict crossed into the house to take the call. The day's pleasure disappeared as she heard the curt tone of his voice, saw him make notes on paper then fold the sheet into his shirt pocket.

Nice plans, she thought with wistful regret as she cleared their breakfast dishes onto a tray and carried them through to the kitchen. Pity they had to be abandoned.

She was determined not to show her disappointment. 'Shall I take more coffee through to the study?'

He shot her a sharp look. 'I need an hour, maybe less. Then we'll leave.'

'Can I help?'

He gave a brief nod of assent, and she followed him to the study.

The fax machine held paper, and Benedict collected it *en route* to the desk. Within seconds the laptop was up and running.

They worked together side by side and, when the document was done and checked, it was consigned to the printer then faxed through to the States.

'OK. Let's get out of here.'

Five minutes later Benedict reversed the four-wheel drive from the garage and, once clear of suburbia, he headed west, taking the mountain road to Mount Tamborine.

'Thanks.'

'Whatever for?'

The terrain was lush green after seasonal subtropical rain. Grassed paddocks, bush-clad hills, homes on acreage, working farms.

They were gaining height as the bitumen road curved round the foothills and began its snaking ascent towards the peak.

'The weekend,' Gabbi elaborated. 'Today.' For the simple pleasures that cost only his time and therefore were infinitely more precious to her than anything money could buy.

'It's not over yet.'

No. The sun suddenly appeared much brighter, the sky a magical azure.

As the road wound higher there was a spectacular view of the hinterland, and in the distance lay the ocean, a sapphire jewel.

They reached the uppermost peak and travelled the road that traversed its crest, past houses of various ages and designs, an old-English-style hotel, and a quaint café.

The village was a mixture of shops with broad verandahs clumped together, and they stopped to purchase a large bottle of chilled mineral water, some delicious ham and salad rolls and fruit. Then they walked back to the four-wheel drive and drove to a grassed reserve with magnificent views over the valley.

It was isolated, picturesque, and Gabbi felt as if they were perched on top of the world, removed from everything and everyone. It was a heady feeling, more intoxicating than wine, breathtaking.

Benedict unfolded a rug and spread it over the grass beneath the shade of a nearby tree. They ate until they were replete then sprawled comfortably, at ease with the vista and the silence.

A true picnic, it reminded Gabbi of the many she'd shared with Jacques in the days when laughter had risen readily to her lips and the only cares she had had were studying and excelling in her exams.

'Penny for them.'

Gabbi turned at the sound of Benedict's drawling voice, and gave him a slow smile. 'We should do this more often.'

'That's it?'

He sounded mildly amused, but she could play the faintly teasing game as well as he. 'You want my innermost thoughts?'

'It would be a start.'

'I love you' was so easy to say, so difficult to retract. Whispered in the deep night hours was one thing—voiced in the early afternoon on a mountain-top was something else.

'I was thinking this is a little piece of heaven,' she

said lightly. 'Far away from the city, business pressures, people.'

'The place, or the fact we're sharing it?'

She offered him a wide smile that reached her eyes and lit them as vividly as the blue of the ocean in the distance. 'Why, *both*, of course. It wouldn't be nearly as much fun on my own.'

He curled a hand beneath her nape and brought his mouth down over hers in an evocative kiss that teased, tantalised and stopped just short of total possession.

'Witch,' he murmured a few moments later against her temple. 'Do you want to stay here, or explore the mountain further?'

She pressed a kiss to the hollow at the base of his throat and savoured the faint taste that was his alone—male heat mingled with cleanliness and exclusive cologne.

'We're close to a public road, it's a public park, and we wouldn't want to shock anyone passing by,' she teased, using the edge of her teeth to nip his skin. 'Besides, there's a plane waiting to take us back to the rat race.'

'Tomorrow morning. Dawn.'

They had the night. 'We shouldn't waste a moment,' Gabbi said with mock reverence, and gave his chest a gentle push. 'When we reach the coast we'll get some prawns and Moreton Bay bugs which you can cook on the barbecue while I get a salad together. We'll open a bottle of wine, eat, and watch the sun go down.'

He let her go, watched as she rose lithely to her

feet, then took her outstretched hand and levered himself upright in one fluid movement.

It was after five when they entered the house, and by tacit agreement they took a long walk over the damp, packed sand of an outgoing tide, then reluctantly turned and retraced their steps.

Her hand was held lightly clasped in his, and a faint breeze tugged her blouse and teased loose tendrils free from the careless knot of her hair. Her skin glowed from its exposure to the fresh sea air, and her eyes held a mystic depth that owed much to the pleasure of the day, and the anticipation of the night.

After preparing the meal there was time to change into swimwear and swim several lengths of the pool before emerging to dry the excess water from their skin.

The aroma of barbecued seafood heightened their appetite, and, seated out on the terrace, Gabbi reached for a prawn with her fingers, declared it ambrosia, then reached for another as she dug her fork into a delectable portion of salad.

'You've got prawn juice on your chin,' Benedict said lazily, and she directed a dazzling smile at him.

'Terribly inelegant.' She tore flesh from the shell of a perfectly cooked bug and ate it in slow, delicate bites. Monique would have been appalled. There wasn't a lemon-scented fingerbowl in sight. And paper napkins weren't an accepted substitute for fine Irish linen.

The sun began to sink, and the light dimmed, streaking the sky to the west with reflected pink that slowly changed to orange, a brilliant flare of colour that slowly faded, then disappeared, leaving behind a dusky glow.

Timed lights sprang up around the pool, lit the terrace, and cast a reflection that was almost ethereal until darkness fell and obliterated everything beyond their immediate line of vision.

Gabbi heard the phone, and watched as Benedict rose from his chair to answer it. She gathered the seafood debris together, stacked plates onto the tray, took it indoors to the electronic food trolley, then pressed the button that lifted it up to the kitchen. Then she closed the doors onto the terrace and activated the security system.

Dishes and cutlery were dispensed into the dishwasher, the kitchen soon restored to order. Her hair had long since dried, but needed to be rinsed of chlorine from the pool, and she made her way upstairs to the shower.

Afterwards she donned briefs, pulled on long white trousers in a soft cheesecloth, then added a matching sleeveless button-through blouse. Several minutes with the hair-drier removed the excess moisture from her hair, and she left it loose, added a touch of lip-gloss, then ran lightly down to the kitchen.

Coffee. Hot, strong and black, with a dash of liqueur.

The coffee had just finished filtering into the glass carafe when Benedict joined her, and she cast him a searching look.

'Problems?'

'Nothing I can't handle.'

She didn't doubt it. She poured the brew into a cup and handed it to him. 'Need me?'

His eyes flared. 'Yes.' His implication was unmistakable, and her heart skipped a beat, quickened, then slowly settled. 'But right now I have to make a series of phone calls.' He lowered his head and took her mouth in a soft kiss that made her ache for more. Then he turned and made his way across the landing to the study.

Gabbi took her coffee into the lounge, settled in a comfortable settee and switched on the television set. Cable TV ensured instant entertainment to satisfy every whim, and she flicked through the channels until she found a sitcom that promised lightness and mirth.

One programme ran into another, and she fought against an increasing drowsiness, succumbing without conscious effort.

There was a vague feeling of being held in strong arms, the sensation of being divested of her outer clothes, then the softness of a pillow beneath her cheek, and a warm body moulded against her back.

CHAPTER EIGHT

THE Lear jet turned off the runway and cruised slowly into a private parking bay at Sydney's domestic airport.

Serg was waiting with the Bentley, and after transferring overnight bags into the boot he slipped behind the wheel and headed the car towards the eastern suburbs.

Gabbi sank back against the leather cushioning and viewed the scene beyond the windscreen. Traffic was already building up, clogging the main arterial roads as commuters drove to their places of work.

In an hour she'd join them. She looked at her casual cotton shirt, trousers and trainers. Soon she'd exchange them for a suit, tights and high heels.

Even now she could sense Benedict withdrawing, his mind already preoccupied with business and the day ahead.

Marie served breakfast within minutes of their arrival home, and shortly after eight Gabbi slid behind the wheel of her car and trailed Benedict's Bentley down the drive.

The day was uneventful, although busy, and lunch was something she sent out for and ate at her desk. Waiting for a faxed confirmation and acting on it provided an unwanted delay, and consequently it was almost six when she garaged the car.

While Monique took liberties with time as a guest, as a hostess she insisted on punctuality. Six-thirty for seven meant exactly that. Which left Gabbi twenty minutes in which to shower, dress, apply make-up and tend to her hair.

She began unbuttoning her suit jacket as she raced up the stairs, hopping from one foot to the other as she paused to remove her heeled pumps. By the time she reached the bedroom she'd released the zip-fastener of her skirt and her fingers were busy with the buttons on her blouse.

Benedict looked up from applying the electric razor to a day's growth of beard and raised an enquiring eyebrow as she entered the *en suite* bathroom.

'Don't ask,' Gabbi flung at him as she slid open the shower door and turned on the water.

Black silk evening trousers, a matching singlet top and a black beaded jacket. High-heeled black pumps. Gold jewellery. Hair swept on top of her head, light make-up with emphasis on the eyes.

Gabbi didn't even think, she just went with it, relying on speed and dexterity for a finished result which, she accepted with a cursory glance in the cheval-glass, would pass muster.

She reached for her evening bag, pushed its long gold chain over one shoulder and turned to see Benedict regarding her with a degree of lazy amusement.

'No one would guess you achieved that result in so short a time,' he commented as they descended the staircase and made their way to the garage.

'I'll take three deep breaths in the car and think pleasant thoughts.'

She did. Not that it helped much. With every passing kilometre the nerves inside her stomach intensified, which was foolish, for Annaliese was unlikely to misbehave in Monique and James's presence.

'Darlings.' Annaliese greeted them individually with a kiss to both cheeks. 'Two of my favourite people.' Her smile was stunning as she moved between Gabbi and Benedict and linked an arm through each of theirs. 'Come through to the lounge.'

One eyebrow slanted as she ruefully glanced from Gabbi's black evening suit to her own figure-moulding black cocktail gown. 'Great minds, darling?' The light tinkling laugh held humour that failed to reach her eyes. 'We always did have an extraordinarily similar taste in clothes.'

Except I paid for my own, while you racked up Alaia and Calvin Klein on James's credit card, Gabbi added silently. *Stop it,* she chided herself.

Her father's home was beautiful, tastefully if expensively decorated, and a superb show-case for a man of James's wealth and social position. Why, then, did she feel uncomfortable every time she stepped inside the door? Was it because Monique had carefully redecorated, systematically replacing drapes, subtly altering colour schemes, until almost every memory of Gabbi's mother had been removed?

Yet why shouldn't Monique impose her own taste? James had obviously been willing to indulge her. And the past, no matter how idyllic a memory, had little place in today's reality.

'Gabbi. Benedict.' Monique moved towards them with both hands outstretched. 'I was afraid you were going to be late.'

James gave his daughter a hug and laid a hand on Benedict's arm. 'Come and sit down. I'll get you both a drink.'

Innocuous social small talk. They were each adept at the art—the smiles, the laughter. To an outsider they resembled a happy, united family, Gabbi reflected as she took a seat next to Benedict at the dining table.

Monique's cook had prepared exquisitely presented courses that tantalised the taste buds. Tonight she excelled with *vichyssoise verte* as a starter.

'We arranged an impromptu tennis evening last night,' Monique revealed as they finished the soup. 'I put a call through, hoping you might be able to join us, but Marie informed me that you were away for the weekend.'

Monique possessed the ability to phrase a statement so that it resembled a question, and Gabbi fingered the stem of her water-glass, then chose to lift it to her lips.

'We flew to the coast,' Benedict drawled in response.

'Really?' Annaliese directed a brilliant smile at Gabbi. 'I'm surprised you were able to drag Benedict away from Sydney.' She switched her attention to Benedict and the smile became coquettish. 'I thought it was a requisite of the corporate wife to be able to entertain herself.'

Gabbi replaced her glass carefully. 'Surely not to

the exclusion of spending quality time with her husband?'

The cook served a superb *poulet français*, with accompanying vegetables.

'Of course not, darling.' Annaliese proffered a condescending smile. 'It was very thoughtful of Benedict to indulge you.'

Gabbi picked up her cutlery and speared her portion of chicken, then she sliced a bite-size piece with delicate precision. 'Yes, wasn't it?' She forked the morsel into her mouth, savoured it, then offered a compliment that the chef deserved. 'This is delicious, Monique.'

'Thank you, Gabrielle.'

Gabbi completed a mental count to three. Any second now Monique would instigate a subtle third degree.

'I trust you had an enjoyable time?'

'It was very relaxing.'

'Did you take in a show at the Casino?'

'No,' Benedict intervened. 'Gabbi cooked dinner and we stayed home.' He turned towards Gabbi with a warm intimate smile which melted her bones.

Great, Gabbi sighed silently. You've taken control of Monique's game, and provided Annaliese with the ammunition to fire another round.

'You never cooked at home, darling.' The tinkling laugh was without humour.

'There was no need. We always had a chef to prepare meals.' Besides, Monique hadn't wanted her in the kitchen, even on the chef's night off.

'It could have been arranged, Gabbi.'

She looked at James and smiled. 'It was never that important.'

'You should give us the opportunity to sample your culinary efforts, Gabrielle.'

After all these years, Monique? 'I wouldn't think of hurting Marie's feelings by suggesting I usurp her position in the kitchen.'

'Marie *does* have a night off, darling,' Annaliese remonstrated in faintly bored tones.

'Yes,' she responded evenly. 'On the evenings Benedict and I eat out.'

Her stepsister examined the perfection of her lacquered nails, then spared Gabbi a teasing smile. 'You're hedging at extending an invitation.'

Venom, packaged in velvet and presented with pseudo-sincerity. Gabbi handled it with the ease of long practice. 'Not at all. Which evening would suit?'

It was a polite battle, but a battle nonetheless.

'Monique? James?' Annaliese was gracious in her deferral.

'Can I check my diary, darling, and get back to you?'

Gabbi was equally gracious. 'Of course.'

'I'm intrigued to learn what you will serve,' Annaliese purred.

'Marie can always be guaranteed to present an excellent meal,' Gabbi supplied, determined not to be backed into a corner.

Monique's eyes narrowed, as did her daughter's, and each man picked up on the tension, electing to defuse it by initiating a discussion totally unrelated to social niceties.

Bombe au chocolat was served for dessert. Afterwards they retired to the lounge for coffee.

'I thought we might play cards,' Monique suggested. 'Poker?'

'As long as it's not strip poker,' Annaliese teased with a provocative smile. 'I'll lose every stitch I'm wearing.'

And love every minute of it, Gabbi thought hatefully.

'We close the table at eleven-thirty. Winning hand takes the pool.' James deferred to Benedict. 'Agreed?'

'Agreed.'

The game wasn't about skill or luck, winning or losing. The stakes were minuscule, the ensuing two hours merely entertainment.

Annaliese seemed to delight in leaning forward at every opportunity in a deliberate attempt to display the delicate curve of her breasts and the fact that she wore nothing to support them.

Add a tantalising smile and sparkling witchery every time she looked at Benedict and Gabbi was feeling positively feral by the time the evening drew to a close.

'No comment?' Benedict ventured as he drove through the gates and turned onto the road.

Gabbi drew a deep breath then released it slowly. 'Where would you like me to begin?'

He spared her a quizzical glance, then concentrated on merging with the traffic. 'Anywhere will do, as long as you release some of that fine rage.'

'You noticed.'

'I was probably the only one who did.'

'It's such a relief to know that.' Dammit, she wanted to *hit* something.

'Don't,' Benedict cautioned with dangerous softness, and she turned on him at once.

'Don't—*what*?'

'Slam a fist against the dashboard. You'll only hurt yourself.'

'Perhaps I should hit you instead.'

'Want me to pull over, or can it wait until we get home?'

'Don't try to humour me, Benedict.' She focused her attention on the scene beyond the windscreen: the bright headlights of oncoming traffic, fluorescent street-lamps and the elongated shadows they cast in the darkness.

Gabbi hurried indoors as soon as Benedict released the alarm system, not even pausing as he reset it. She made for the foyer and had almost reached the staircase when a hand clamped on her arm.

Any words she might have uttered were stilled as he swung her round and caught her close. There was nothing she could do to halt the descent of his mouth, or deny its possession of her own.

Hard, hungry, almost punishing. It defused her anger, as he meant it to do. And when her body softened and leant in against his he altered the nature of the kiss, deepening it until she clung to him.

A husky groan emerged from her throat as he swung an arm beneath her knees and lifted her into his arms. There wasn't a word she could think of uttering as he carried her up the stairs to their room. Or an action she wanted to take to stop him removing her clothes and his, before he drew her down onto the bed.

A long, slow exploration of the pleasure spots, the touch of his lips against the curve of her calf, the sensitive crease behind her knee, then the evocative path along her inner thigh... Gabbi felt her body begin to melt like wax beneath the onslaught of flame, until she was totally malleable, *his*, to do with as he chose.

Shared intimacy. Mutual sexual gratification. Was that all it was to Benedict?

Love. While her heart craved the words, her head ruled that she should be content without them.

Premium seating tickets for *Phantom of the Opera* were sold out weeks in advance. Benedict had undoubtedly wielded some influence to gain four tickets at such short notice, Gabbi mused as she took her seat beside him.

'Wonderful position,' Francesca murmured as the orchestra began an introductory number prior to the opening of the first act.

'Yes, isn't it?'

'You look stunning in that colour.'

The compliment was genuine, and Gabbi accepted it with a smile. 'Thanks.' Peacock-blue silk shot with green, it highlighted the texture of her skin and emphasised her blonde hair. 'So do you,' she returned warmly.

Deep ruby-red velvet did wonders for Francesca's colouring, and moulded her slim curves to perfection.

The music swelled, the curtain rose, and Act One began.

Gabbi adored the visual dimension of live performance—the presence of the actors, the costumes, the faint smell of greasepaint and make-up, the sounds. It was a totally different experience to film.

The interval between each act allowed sufficient time for patrons to emerge into the foyer for a drink, or a cigarette for those who smoked.

Gabbi expected to see James, Monique and Annaliese in the crowd. What she didn't expect was for Annaliese to readily abandon Monique and James and spend the interval conversing with Francesca, Dominic and Benedict. Apart from a perfunctory greeting, Gabbi was barely acknowledged.

The buzzer sounded its warning for patrons to resume their seats. As soon as the lights dimmed Benedict reached for her hand and held it firmly within his own. At the close of the next act he didn't release it when they stood and moved towards the foyer.

'The powder-room?' Francesca queried, and Gabbi inclined her head in agreement a split second before she caught sight of Annaliese weaving a determined path towards them.

'Fabulous evening,' her stepsister enthused with a dazzling smile.

'Yes, isn't it?' Gabbi agreed as she slipped her hand free. 'If you'll excuse Fran and me for a few minutes?'

'Of course.' Annaliese's delight was almost evident. 'I'll keep Benedict and Dominic amused in your absence.'

And relish every second, Gabbi observed uncharitably.

'Doesn't give up, does she?' Francesca said quietly as she followed Gabbi through the crowd. 'Have you told her to get lost?'

'Yes.' They entered the powder-room and joined the queue.

'The polite version?' Francesca asked. 'Or the no-holds-barred cat-fight rendition?'

'Would you accept icily civil?' Gabbi countered with a smile.

'A little bit of fire wouldn't go amiss. Italians are very good at it.' A wicked gleam lit her eyes. 'We yell, we throw things.'

'I've never seen you in action,' Gabbi said with genuine amusement.

'That's because I've never been mad at you.'

'Heaven forbid.' They moved forward a few paces. 'Dare I ask how things are going between you and Dominic?'

'I shall probably throw something at him soon.'

A bubble of laughter rose in Gabbi's throat. 'Should I warn him, do you think?'

'Let it be a surprise.'

Dominic was a man of Benedict's calibre. Dynamic, compelling, *electrifying*. And mercilessly indomitable in his pursuit of the seemingly unattainable. Gabbi was unsure how much longer Dominic would allow Francesca to maintain an upper hand.

The outcome, she decided with a secret smile, would be interesting.

The buzzer for the commencement of the following act sounded as they freshened their make-up, and they resumed their seats as the lights began to dim.

It was a faultless performance, the singers in excellent voice. As the curtain fell on the final act there was a burst of applause from the audience that succeeded in a further curtain call.

Emerging from the crush of the dispersing crowd took some time.

'Shall we go on somewhere for a light supper?' Dominic asked as they reached the car park.

'Love to,' Gabbi accepted. 'Where do you have in mind?'

'Benedict?'

'Your choice, Dom,' he drawled.

'There's an excellent place at Double Bay.' He named it. 'We'll meet you there.'

'Relax,' Benedict bade Gabbi as the Bentley by-passed the Botanical Gardens. 'I doubt Annaliese will embark on a club crawl in an effort to determine our whereabouts.'

'How astute,' Gabbi congratulated with a degree of mockery. 'Her enthusiasm hasn't escaped you.'

'And you, Gabbi,' he continued, 'are fully aware I provide Annaliese with no encouragement whatsoever.'

'*Darling* Benedict, are you aware that you don't need to?'

'You sound like a jealous wife.'

'Well, of course.'

He slanted her a dark glance and chided softly, 'Don't be facetious.'

Her lips curved to form a wicked smile. 'One has to develop a sense of humour.'

'I could, and probably should, spank you.'

'Do that, and I'll seek my own revenge.'

He gave a husky laugh. 'It might almost be worth it.'

'I think,' Gabbi said judiciously, 'you should give the road your full attention.'

The restaurant was situated above a block of shops on the main Double Bay thoroughfare. The ambience was authentically Greek, and it soon became apparent that Dominic was not only a favoured patron but also a personal friend of the owner.

Gabbi declined strong coffee in favour of tea, and nibbled from a platter filled with a variety of sweet and savory pastries.

Dominic was a skilled raconteur, possessed of a dry sense of humour which frequently brought laughter to Gabbi's lips and, unless she was mistaken, penetrated a chink in Francesca's façade.

It was after midnight when they bade each other goodnight and slid into separate cars, almost one when Gabbi slid between the sheets and Benedict snapped off the bedside lamp.

CHAPTER NINE

STANTON-NICOLS supported a few select charities, and tonight's event was in the form of a prestigious annual dinner held in the banquet room of a prominent city hotel.

Noted as an important occasion among the social élite, it achieved attendance in the region of a thousand patrons.

Haute couture was clearly evident as society doyennes strove to outdo each other, and Gabbi suppressed the wry observation that their jewellery, collectively, would probably fund a starving nation with food.

Men fared much better than women in the fashion stakes. They simply chose a black evening suit, white shirt and black bow-tie, albeit the suit might be Armani or Zegna, the shoes hand-stitched and the shirt expensive pure cotton.

Gabbi had chosen a full-length slimline strapless gown of multicoloured silk organza featuring the muted colours of spring. Cut low at the back, it was complemented by an attached panel and completed by a long, trailing neck-scarf in matching silk organza.

Tonight she'd elected to leave her hair loose, and the carefree windswept style enhanced her attractive features.

Six-thirty for seven allowed time for those who

chose to arrive early to mix and mingle over drinks in the large foyer. The banquet-room doors were opened at seven, and dinner was served thirty minutes later.

'A glass of champagne?'

'Orange juice,' Gabbi decided as a waiter hovered with a tray of partly filled flutes. She removed the appropriate flute and caught the glimmer of amusement apparent in Benedict's dark eyes.

'The need for a clear head?'

Her mouth curved to form a winsome smile. 'You read me well.' James, Monique and Annaliese would be seated at the same table, together with five fellow guests.

'Every time, *querida*,' he mocked softly, and saw the faint dilation of her pupils at his use of the Spanish endearment. Did he know the occasional use of his late mother's native language had the power to stir her emotions?

Her momentary disconcertion was quickly masked as Benedict greeted a colleague, and with skilled ease she engaged in small talk with the colleague's wife for the few minutes until Benedict indicated the necessity to locate their designated table.

Stanton-Nicols was one of several sponsors contributing to the event, and already seated at their table was the charity chairman and his wife and a visiting titled dignitary together with his wife and son.

The five minutes remaining before dinner was served were crucial for those who chose to make an entrance. James, Monique and Annaliese slid into their seats with barely one minute to spare, with the obligatory air-kiss, the smiles and the faint touch of a hand. Perfect, Gabbi noted silently. Monique had done it again, ensuring they were the last to arrive, and their passage, weaving through countless tables, observed by almost everyone in the room.

As the waiters distributed the first of three courses, the compère welcomed the guests, outlined the evening's programme, and thanked everyone for their patronage.

Light background music filtered unobtrusively from numerous speakers as Gabbi lifted her fork and started on an appetising prawn and avocado cocktail.

Someone—Monique, as a dedicated committee member? Gabbi pondered—had seen fit to seat Annaliese on Benedict's left and the visiting titled dignitary's son on Gabbi's right.

The seemingly careless placing of Annaliese's hand on Benedict's thigh during the starter could have been coincidental, although Gabbi doubted it.

'Pleasant evening,' the dignitary's son observed. 'Good turn-out.'

Hardly scintillating conversation, but it provided a necessary distraction, and Gabbi offered a polite rejoinder.

'An interesting mix,' he continued. 'A professional singer and a fashion parade.'

'Plus the obligatory speeches.'

His smile was disarming. 'You've been here before.'

Gabbi's mouth slanted to form a generous curve. 'Numerous times.'

'May I say you look enchanting?'

Her eyes held mild amusement as she took in his kindly features. 'Thank you.'

Their plates were removed, and she offered Benedict a wide smile as he filled her water glass. His eyes were dark, enigmatic, and she pressed a hand on his right thigh. 'Thank you, darling.'

'My pleasure.'

A *double entendre* if ever there was one, and she deliberately held his gaze, silently challenging him.

An announcement by the compère that they were to be entertained with two songs by the guest singer was a timely diversion, and Gabbi listened with polite attention.

The main course was served: chicken Kiev, baby potatoes and an assortment of vegetables.

'Wonderful food,' the dignitary's son declared as he demolished his serving with enthusiasm, and Gabbi tried not to notice Annaliese's scarlet-tipped fingers settling on Benedict's forearm.

The singer performed another medley, which was followed by dessert, then the charity chairman took the podium.

At that point Annaliese slid to her feet and discreetly disappeared to one side of the stage.

Coffee was served as the compère announced the fashion parade, and with professional panache three male and three female models appeared on the catwalk, displaying creations from prominent Sydney designers in a variety of styles ranging from resort, city and career, to designer day, cocktail and formal evening wear.

'Stunning, isn't she?'

Gabbi turned towards the titled dignitary's son and saw his attention was focused on Annaliese's progress down the catwalk. 'Yes.' It was nothing less than the truth. Her stepsister exuded self-confidence and had the height, the body, the face...all the qualities essential for success in the modelling arena.

Most men took one look and were entranced by the visual package; most women recognised the artificiality beneath the flawless figure and exquisite features.

Annaliese participated in each section, her smile practised and serene. Although as the parade progressed it became increasingly obvious that she singled out one table for special attention...one man as the recipient of an incredibly sexy smile.

Gabbi's tension mounted with each successive procession down the catwalk, and it irked her unbearably that she was powerless to do anything about it. Except smile.

Benedict, damn him, took an interest in each model and every item displayed. Resort wear included swimwear. The bikini, the high-cut maillot. Annaliese looked superb in a minuscule bikini...and was well aware of her effect.

Gabbi felt the urge to kill and controlled it. The slightest hint of her displeasure at Annaliese's provocative behaviour would be seen as a victory, and she refused to give her stepsister that satisfaction.

Evening wear provided Annaliese with another opportunity to stun when she appeared in a backless, strapless creation that moulded her curves like a second skin.

The finale brought all the participating models on stage for one last turn on the catwalk.

'Is there anything that catches your eye?' Benedict enquired.

'The tall blond male model,' Gabbi responded with a deliberate smile, and glimpsed the amusement that lightened his features.

'Naturally you refer to the clothes he's wearing.'

She allowed her eyes to widen, and they held a glint of wicked humour. 'Naturally. Although the whole package is very attractive. He was magnificently *impressive* in swimwear.'

'Payback time?'

'Why, Benedict. Whatever do you mean?'

His expression held a degree of lazy tolerance. 'It'll keep.'

'You think so?'

A gleam lit his dark eyes. 'We could always leave and continue this conversation in private.'

'And commit a social *faux pas*?'

With indolent ease he reached for her left hand and raised it to his lips. 'I'm fortunate. I get to take you home.'

He kissed each finger in turn, then enfolded her hand in his on the table. Sensation flared and travelled like flame through her veins, but there was no visible change in his expression except for the crooked smile twitching the edges of his mouth as his thumb traced an idle pattern back and forth across the throbbing pulse at her wrist.

His eyes speared hers, faintly mocking beneath

slightly hooded lids, and the breath caught in her throat.

'Some consolation,' she managed in an attempt at humour.

'The prize.'

She wanted quite desperately for it to be the truth, but she was all too aware it was part of the game. 'Ah,' she said with soft cynicism. 'You say the sweetest things.'

'Gracias.'

The waiters served another round of coffee as guests moved from one table to another, pausing to chat with friends as they made a slow progression towards the foyer.

'I've enjoyed your company.'

Gabbi heard the words and turned towards the dignitary's son. 'Thank you.' She included his parents. 'It's been a pleasant evening.'

'Most pleasant,' James agreed as he moved to his daughter's side and brushed a light kiss over her cheek. 'You look wonderful.'

'Thanks,' she murmured, and endeavoured to keep a smile in place as Annaliese rejoined them.

'A few of us are going on to a nightclub.' Her eyes focused on Benedict as she touched a hand to his shoulder. 'Why don't you join us?'

Gabbi wasn't aware that she held her breath as she waited for his reply.

'Another time perhaps.'

'We must do lunch, Gabrielle,' Monique insisted as she bade them goodnight. 'I'll ring.'

Gabbi felt a sense of remorse at wanting to refuse.

It wasn't very often that her stepmother suggested a *tête-à-tête*. 'Please do.'

It was half an hour before they reached the car park and a further thirty minutes before Benedict brought the Bentley to a halt inside the garage.

'A record attendance,' he commented as they entered the house. 'The committee will be pleased.'

'Yes.'

'You sound less than enthused.'

'I'm disappointed.'

'Explain,' Benedict commanded as he reset the security alarm.

'I was just *dying* to go on to the nightclub.'

He turned and closed the distance between them, and her eyes took on a defiant gleam as he pushed a hand beneath her hair and captured her nape.

'Were you, indeed?'

He was much too close. His cologne teased her nostrils and melded with the musky male fragrance that was his alone.

'Yes. It would have been such *fun* watching Annaliese trying to seduce you.' She lifted a hand and trailed her fingers down the lapel of his suit.

'Your claws are showing.'

'And I thought I was being so subtle.'

'Do you want to debate Annaliese's behaviour?'

Her eyes glittered with inner anger, their depths darkening to deep sapphire. 'I don't think "debate" quite covers it.'

One eyebrow slanted in quizzical humour. 'It's a little late for a punishing set of tennis. Besides, I'd probably win.' His warm breath teased the tendrils of hair drifting close to one ear. 'And that,' he persisted quietly, 'wouldn't be the object of the exercise, would it?'

She wanted to generate a reaction that would allow her to vent her own indignation. 'At least I'd get some satisfaction from thrashing the ball with a racquet.'

His eyes were dark, fathomless. 'I can think of a far more productive way to expend all that pent-up energy.'

A thumb traced the edge of her jaw, then trailed lightly down the pulsing cord of her neck.

Gabbi could feel the insidious warmth spread through her veins, her skin begin to tingle as fine body hair rose in anticipation of his touch. 'You're not playing fair.'

He lowered his head and brushed his lips against her temple. 'I'm not *playing* at anything.'

Gabbi closed her eyes and absorbed the intoxicating feel of him as he angled his mouth over her own. His fingers tangled in her hair as he steadily deepened the kiss, intensifying the slow, burning heat of her arousal until it threatened to rage out of control.

Her body strained against his, pulsing, needing so much more, and she was hardly conscious of the small, encouraging sounds low in her throat as she urged him on.

Slowly, gently, he eased back and broke the contact, then swept an arm beneath her knees and crossed the foyer to the stairs.

'The bedroom is so civilised,' Gabbi breathed softly as she traced the lobe of his ear with her tongue and gently bit its centre.

When they reached their suite the door closed behind them with a satisfying clunk. 'You want *uncivilised*, Gabbi?' he demanded as he let her slide down to her feet.

The words conjured up a mental image so evocatively erotic that she had to fight to control the jolt of feeling that surged through her body.

'This is a very expensive gown,' she announced in a dismal attempt at flippancy. 'One I'd like to wear again.'

Something leapt in his eyes and remained there. A dark, primitive glitter that momentarily arrested the thudding beat of her heart before it kicked in at a wildly accelerated pace.

The breath caught in her throat as he reached for the zip-fastening and freed it so that the gown slid down to the carpet. With mesmerised fascination she stepped aside and watched as he carelessly tossed it over a nearby chair.

His eyes never left hers as he traced the swell of her breasts, teased each sensitive peak, then slowly slipped his fingers beneath the band of her briefs and slid them to her feet.

Her evening sandals came next, and she watched as he removed his jacket and tossed it across the valet-frame.

The bow-tie followed, and his shirt. Shoes and socks were abandoned, and his trousers landed on top of his jacket.

Then he captured her face in his hands and lowered his mouth to hers, initiating a kiss that took possession and demanded complete capitulation.

This was no seduction. It was claim-staking. Ruthless hunger and treacherous devastation.

She didn't fight it. Didn't want to. She rode the crest of his passion, and exulted in the ravishment of unleashed emotions.

It became a ravaging of body and mind—hers—as she gave herself up to him, her surrender complete as he tasted and suckled, tormenting her to the point of madness.

She had no control over her shuddering body, or the way it convulsed in the storm of her own passion. And she was completely unaware of the emotional sobs tearing free from her throat as she begged him not to stop.

A beautiful way to die, Gabbi decided with dizzying certainty as he dragged her down onto the bed. Then she was conscious only of unspeakable pleasure as he drove himself into her, again and again, deeper and deeper as she arched up to him in a dark, rhythmic beat that flung them both over the edge.

Afterwards she lay in a tangle of sheets, her limbs entwined with his, disinclined to move.

She didn't have the energy to lift a hand, and her eyes remained closed, for to open them required too much effort.

'Did I hurt you?'

She ached. Dear God, *how* she ached. But it was with acute pleasure, not pain. 'No.' A soft smile curved her lips. 'Although I don't think I'm ready for an encore just yet.'

He leaned forward and pressed a lingering kiss to the sensitive hollow at the base of her throat, then trailed a path to the edge of her mouth. 'Relax, *querida*. It's not an act I could follow too soon.'

'Some act.'

She felt him move, and the sheet settled down onto soft, highly sensitised skin. She sighed and let her head settle into the curve of his shoulder. Heaven didn't get any better than this.

Gabbi woke to the touch of lips brushing against her cheek, and she stretched, arching the slim bow of her body like a contented feline beneath the stroke of its master.

A smile teased her mouth and she let her eyes drift open.

'Is it late?'

'Late enough, *querida*.'

He was dressed, shaven and, unless she was mistaken, ready to leave.

Regret tinged her expression. 'I was going to drive with you to the airport.'

'Instead you can relax in the Jacuzzi, enjoy a leisurely breakfast and scan the newspaper before going in to the office.'

'You should have woken me,' she protested, and saw the gleam of humour evident in the dark eyes above her own.

'I just have.' He indicated a tray on the bedside pedestal. 'And brought orange juice and coffee.'

She eased herself into a sitting position and hugged her knees. A mischievous twinkle lightened her eyes. 'In that case, you're forgiven.'

'You can reach me on my mobile phone.'

He had assumed the mantle of business executive along with the three-piece suit. His mind, she knew, was already on the first of several meetings scheduled over the next few days in Melbourne.

She reached for the orange juice and took a long swallow, grateful for the refreshing, cool taste of freshly squeezed juice.

She'd wanted to wake early, share a slow loving, join him in the Jacuzzi and linger over breakfast. Now she had to settle for a swift kiss and watch him walk out the door.

The kiss was more than she'd hoped for, but less than she needed, and her eyes were wistful as he disappeared from the room.

Four days, three nights. Hardly any time at all. He'd been gone for much longer in the past. Why now did she place such emphasis on his absence?

She finished the orange juice, slid from the bed and made for the bathroom. Half an hour later she ran lightly down the stairs and made her way to the kitchen.

'Morning, Marie.'

The housekeeper's smile held genuine warmth. 'Good morning. Do you want to eat inside, or on the terrace?'

'The terrace,' Gabbi answered promptly.

'Cereal and fruit, toast, coffee? Or would you prefer a cooked breakfast?'

'Cereal, thanks. I'll get it.' She plucked a bowl from the cupboard, retrieved the appropriate cereal container, added a banana, extracted milk from the refrigerator then moved through the wide sliding glass doors that led out onto the terrace.

The sun was warm on her skin, despite the early-morning hour. It would be all too easy to banish work from the day, stay home and spend several lazy hours reading a book beneath the shade of an umbrella...

CHAPTER TEN

'SERG asked me to remind you to take the Bentley this morning.'

Gabbi looked up from scanning the daily newspaper and placed her cup down onto its saucer. She offered Marie a teasing smile. 'Not the XJ220?'

'We won't give him a heart attack,' Marie responded dryly, and Gabbi laughed.

'No, let's not.' The powerful sports car might be Benedict's possession, but it was Serg's pride and joy. Together with the Bentley and Mercedes, he ensured it was immaculately maintained. If the engine of any one of them didn't purr to his satisfaction, he organised a mechanical check-up. For the next few days the Mercedes would be in the panel shop having a new tail-light fitted and the scratches painted over.

The telephone rang, and Marie crossed to answer it. 'Nicols residence.' A few seconds later she covered the mouthpiece and held out the receiver. 'It's for you. Mrs Stanton.'

Gabbi rolled her eyes and rose to her feet to take the call. 'Monique. How are you?'

'Fine, Gabrielle. I thought we might do lunch today. Is that suitable?'

Exchanging social chit-chat with her stepmother over iced water and a lettuce leaf didn't rank high on her list of favoured pastimes. There had to be a reason

for the invitation, and doubtless she'd find out what
it was soon enough.

'Of course,' she responded politely. 'What time,
and where shall I meet you?'

Monique named an exclusive establishment not too
far from Stanton-Nicols Towers. 'Twelve-thirty, darling?'

'I'll look forward to it.' Oh, my, how you lie, an
inner voice taunted. No, that wasn't strictly fair. Life
was full of interesting experiences. Her relationship
with Monique just happened to be one of them.

The traffic was heavy, drivers seemed more impatient than usual, and an accident at an intersection
banked up a line of cars for several kilometres.

Consequently Gabbi was late, there was a message
to say her secretary had reported in sick and the courier bag failed to contain promised documentation.
Not an auspicious start to the day, she decided as she
made the first of several phone calls.

By mid-morning she'd elicited a promise that the
missing documentation would arrive in the afternoon
courier delivery. It meant the loss of several hours,
and if she was to assemble the figures, check and col-
late them for the board meeting tomorrow she'd need
to work late, take work home or come in early in the
morning.

Lunch with Monique loomed close, and with a resigned sigh she closed down the computer and re-
treated to the powder-room to repair her make-up.

Ten minutes later she emerged from the building
and set out at a brisk pace, reaching the restaurant
with less than a minute to spare.

Gabbi followed the maître d' to Monique's table and slid into the seat he held out.

'Gabrielle.'

'Monique.'

Superficial warmth, artificial affection. Ten years down the track, Gabbi was resigned to it never being any different.

As always, Monique was perfectly groomed, with co-ordinated accessories. Chanel bag, Magli shoes, and a few pieces of expensive jewellery. Tasteful, but not ostentatious.

'Annaliese will join us. I hope you don't mind?'

Wonderful. 'Of course not,' she responded politely, and ordered mineral water from the hovering drinks waiter.

'Annaliese felt you might appreciate some family support while Benedict is away.'

Gabbi doubted it very much. The only person Annaliese considered was herself. 'How thoughtful.'

'The banquet dinner was very enjoyable.'

As a conversational gambit, it was entirely neutral. 'A well-presented menu,' she agreed. 'And the fashion parade was excellent.'

'Shall we order a starter? Annaliese might be late.'

Annaliese rarely arrived on time, so why should today be any different? Gabbi settled on avocado with diced mango served on lettuce, then took a sip of mineral water.

'I've managed to persuade James to take a holiday,' Monique began as they waited for their starters.

'What a good idea. When?'

'Next month. A cruise. The *QEII*. We'll pick it up in New York.'

The cruise would be relaxing for James, and sufficiently social to please Monique. 'How long do you plan on being away?'

'Almost three weeks, including flights and stopovers.'

'It'll be a nice break for you both.' And well deserved for her father, whose devotion to Stanton-Nicols' continued success extended way beyond the nine-to-five, five-day-a-week routine.

Their starters arrived, and they were awaiting the main course when Annaliese sauntered up to the table in a cloud of perfume.

'The showing went way over time,' she offered as she sank into the chair opposite her mother. Two waiters hovered solicitously while she made a selection, then each received a haughty dismissal. As soon as they were out of earshot she turned towards Gabbi.

'How are you managing without Benedict?'

The temptation to elaborate was irresistible. 'With great difficulty.'

Annaliese's eyes narrowed fractionally. 'If you were so—' She paused, then went on to add with deliberate emphasis, 'So desperate, you could have accompanied him.'

Gabbi determined to even the score. 'It's not always easy to co-ordinate time away together.'

Annaliese picked up her water-glass and took a delicate sip. 'Really, darling? Why?' She replaced the glass down on the table. 'Everyone knows you hold a token job and take a sizeable salary from a company which regards your services as superfluous.'

Two down. This wasn't looking good. And she was hampered from entering into a verbal cat-fight by Monique's presence.

'My qualifications earned me the token job and standard salary from in excess of twenty applicants,' she declared coolly, knowing she didn't need to justify anything. However, the barb had struck a vulnerable target. 'At the time, James made it very clear his final choice was based entirely on proven results and performance.'

'You expect me to believe he didn't wield any influence?'

It was time to end this, and end it cleanly. 'The directorial board would never sanction wasting company funds on a manufactured position.' Her gaze was level, with only a hint of carefully banked anger apparent.

She wanted to get up and leave, but a degree of courtesy and innate good manners ensured she stayed for the main course and coffee. The food was superb, but her appetite had disappeared, and there was a heaviness at her temple that signalled the onset of a headache.

As soon as she finished her coffee she extracted a credit card from her bag.

'Put that away, Gabrielle,' Monique instructed. 'You're my guest.'

'Thank you. Would you excuse me? I have a two o'clock appointment.'

Annaliese lifted one eyebrow in silent derision, then opined, 'Such dedication.'

'Consideration,' Gabbi corrected her quietly as she rose to her feet. 'To a client-company representative's known punctuality.'

As an exit note it served her reasonably well.

A pity Monique had been present, Gabbi mused as she walked back to the office. On a one-to-one with Annaliese she would have fared much better.

On her return, she found a single red rose in an elegant crystal vase on her desk, along with a white embossed envelope.

Gabbi tore it open and removed the card: 'Missing you. Benedict.'

Not as much as I miss you, she vowed silently as she bent to smell the sweet fragrance from the tight bud.

Tomorrow he would be home. She'd consult with Marie and arrange a special dinner *à deux*. Candles, fine wine, soft music. And afterwards...

The buzz of the intercom brought her back to the present, and she leaned across the desk and depressed the button.

'Michelle Bouchet is waiting in Reception.'

'Thanks, Halle. Have Katherine bring her down.'

Gabbi replaced the receiver and lifted a hand to ease the faint throbbing at her temple. A soft curse left her lips as she caught sight of the time.

It would take at least an hour before she finished reviewing the files on her desk, and a further thirty minutes to log them into the computer.

There were two options. She could take the files and the computer disk home and complete the work there, or she could stay on.

Let's face it, what did she have to rush home for? Besides, Annaliese's deliberate barbs had found their mark.

The decision made, she placed a call through to Marie and let her know she'd be late. Then she sent out for coffee, took two headache tablets and set to work.

It was almost seven when Gabbi exited the program and shut down the computer. Freshly printed pages were collated ready for presentation, and there was satisfaction in knowing the board would be pleased with her analysis.

She collected her bag and vacated the office, bade the attending floor-security officer a polite goodnight, then when the lift arrived she stepped into the cubicle and programmed it for the underground car park.

A swim in the pool, she decided as the lift descended in electronic silence. Followed by a long hot shower. Then she'd settle for a plate of chicken salad, watch television and retire to bed with a book.

The lift came to a halt, and she stepped out as soon as the doors slid open. The car park was well lit, and there were still a number of cars remaining in reserved bays. Executives tying up the day's business, appointments running over time. Dedication to their employer, a determination to earn the mighty dollar? Most likely the latter, Gabbi mused as she walked towards the Bentley.

Deactivating the alarm system, she released the locking mechanism and depressed the door-handle.

'Quietly, miss.' The voice was male, the command ominously soft.

She felt something hard press against her ribs in the same instant that a hand closed over her arm.

'Don't scream, don't struggle and you won't get hurt.'

'Take my bag.' Her voice was cool, calm, although her heart was hammering inside her ribs. 'Take the car.'

The rear door was wrenched open. 'Get in.'

He was going to *kidnap* her? Images flashed through her brain, none of which were reassuring. Dammit, she wasn't going *meekly*. 'No.'

'Listen, sweetheart,' the voice whispered coldly against her ear. 'We don't want anything except a few photos.'

'We'. So there was more than one. It narrowed her chances considerably.

'Now, you can co-operate and make it easy on yourself, or you can fight and get hurt.'

Hands pushed her unceremoniously onto the rear seat, and she gasped out loud as he came down on top of her.

'Get off me!'

Hands found her blouse and ripped it open. Gabbi fought like a wildcat, only to cry out in pain as first one wrist was caught, then the other, and they were held together in a merciless grip. She felt a savage tug as her bra was dragged down, and she twisted her head in a desperate bid to escape his mouth.

Her strength didn't match his, and an outraged growl sounded low in her throat as he ground his teeth against her lips.

Lights flashed as she twisted against him, and when he freed her hands she reached for his head, raking her nails against his scalp and down the side of his neck.

'You bitch!'

He lowered his mouth to her breast and bit hard.

It hurt like hell. Sheer rage and divine assistance allowed her to succeed in manoeuvring her knee between his legs. The tight, upward jerk brought forth an anguished howl and a stream of incomprehensible epithets.

Then Gabbi heard the opposite door open, and two hands dragged her assailant out of the car.

'Come on, man. Let's get the hell out of here. I've got what I need.'

'Bloody little wildcat. I'm going to get her!'

'You were told to rough her up a little. Nothing else. *Remember*?' The door shut with a refined clunk, and Gabbi pulled the door closest to her closed and hit the central locking mechanism.

Then she wriggled over the centre console and slid into the driver's seat. The keys. Where were the keys? Oh, God, they were probably still in the lock.

The two men were walking quickly, one not quite as steadily as the other, and she watched them get into a van, heard the engine roar into life, then speed towards the exit ramp.

Only when the van was out of sight did she lower the car window and retrieve the keys.

Her blouse still gaped open, and she secured it as best she could. She was shaking so badly it took two attempts to insert the ignition key, then she fired the engine and eased the Bentley onto ground level.

Gabbi focused on the traffic, glad for once that there was so much of it. Cars, buses, trucks. Noise. People. They made her feel safe.

Home. She had never felt more grateful to reach the security of Benedict's palatial Vaucluse mansion.

Marie and Serg would be in their flat, and she had no intention of alarming them. Once indoors, she went straight upstairs to the bedroom and removed her clothes. Skirt, torn blouse, underwear. She bundled them together ready for disposal into the rubbish bin. She never wanted to see them again.

Then Gabbi went into the *en suite* bathroom and ran the shower. How long she stayed beneath the stream of water she wasn't sure. She only knew she scrubbed every inch of skin twice over, shampooed her hair not once, but three times. Then she stood still and let the water cascade over her gleaming skin.

Who? *Why?* The questions repeated themselves over and over in her brain as she replayed the scene again and again. Photos. *Blackmail?* The idea seemed ludicrous. Who would want to threaten her? What would they have to gain?

Then other words intruded…and she stood still, examining each one slowly with a sense of growing disbelief.

'You were told to rough her up a little. Nothing else. *Remember?*'

Who would want to frighten but not hurt her? *Dared* not harm her, to give such explicit instructions?

Gabbi shook her head as if to clear it. Photos. Damning shots taken with a specific purpose in mind.

Annaliese. Even her stepsister wouldn't go to such lengths... Would she?

Slowly Gabbi reached out and turned off the water. Then she froze. Someone was in the bedroom.

'Gabbi?'

Benedict.

She swayed, and put out a hand to steady herself. He couldn't be home. He wasn't due back until tomorrow. In a gesture born of desperation she reached for a towel and secured it above her breasts as he entered the *en suite* bathroom.

Her eyes skidded over his tall frame, registered his smile, and glimpsed the faint narrowing of his dark gaze as it swept over her features.

'You're back early.' Dear God. She had to get a grip on herself.

She was too pale, her eyes too dark, dilated and wide, and it was almost impossible to still the faint trembling of her mouth. Without benefit of make-up and a few essential seconds in which to adopt a nonchalant air, she didn't stand a chance.

His silence was ominous, filling the room until she felt like screaming for him to break it.

When he did, she almost wished he hadn't, for his voice was so quiet it turned the blood in her veins to ice.

'What happened?' No preamble, just a chilling demand that brooked no evasion.

Was she so transparent that he had only to take one look? she wondered. She fingered the towel, and fixed her attention on the knot of his impeccable silk tie. 'How was the flight?'

'It doesn't matter a damn in hell about the flight,' he dismissed with lethal softness. *'Tell me.'*

She heard the tension in his voice and was aware there was no easy way to say the words. 'I stayed back at the office to work on some figures.'

His eyes never left hers. 'Why did you do that, when you could easily have brought the disk home?'

Good question. Why *had* she? She swallowed, and saw his eyes follow the movement at her throat.

'Someone slipped through car park security.'

'Are you hurt?' The words held a deadly softness, and a tremor shook her body as his eyes raked every visible inch of her slender frame.

She lifted a hand, then let it fall. 'A few bruises.' He'd see evidence of them soon enough.

'Slowly, Gabbi,' Benedict bit out softly. He reached out a hand and soothed her cheek with his palm. 'From the beginning. And don't omit a single detail.'

His anger was palpable, and she felt afraid. Not for herself. But fearful of what might happen should that anger slip free.

'I unlocked the car door,' she revealed steadily. 'Then someone grabbed me from behind and pushed me onto the rear seat.'

'Don't stop there.' His voice sounded like the swish of a whip, and she flinched as if its tip had flayed her skin.

'He climbed in after me.'

A muscle tensed at the edge of his jaw. 'Did he touch you?'

She shivered at the memory of those brutal fingers manacling her wrists while he ripped open her blouse.

'Not the way you mean.'

Benedict's eyes hardened. 'You called the police?'

She shook her head. 'Nothing was stolen. The car wasn't damaged. I wasn't assaulted.'

His hands settled on her shoulders and slid gently down her arms. 'Assault is a multi-faceted term.' His fingers were incredibly gentle and thorough. Her breath caught when he touched her wrists, and she flinched as he carefully examined first one then the other before raising them to his lips.

His hands reached for the towel, and she froze, all too aware of several deep pink smudges darkening the paleness of her breasts.

Naked fury darkened his features, and his hands clenched until the knuckles showed white.

Gabbi registered dimly that she had wanted to test his control and break it. But never like this.

'I scratched him rather badly,' she offered in explanation. 'And he retaliated.'

There was something primitive in his expression, a stark ruthlessness that frightened her. She needed to diminish it to something approaching civilised restraint. 'His purpose wasn't to harm me. He had an accomplice with a camera.'

Dark, nearly black eyes assumed an almost predatory alertness.

The shrill sound of the telephone made her jump,

and she stared in mesmerised fascination at the bath-room extension.

'Pick it up when I lift the bedroom connection.'

Each word was a harsh directive she didn't think to ignore, and she watched, wide-eyed, as Benedict quickly crossed to the bedside pedestal. Her move-ments synchronised with his, she reached out and lifted the receiver.

'Gabbi Nicols.'

'Gabrielle.' Her name was a distinctive purr on the line, and Gabbi's fingers tightened measurably.

'Annaliese,' she greeted cautiously.

'I have in my possession photos which show you in a state of remarkable *déshabillé*, *mon enfant*.' It was almost possible to *see* Annaliese's cruel smile. 'Copies of them will be despatched to Benedict by courier an hour after his return tomorrow. Together with a file on Tony detailing his career as a profes-sional escort.' She paused, then added with delicate emphasis, 'And listing other services he's only too willing to provide for a price.'

Gabbi felt sick at the thought of being a victim of so much hatred.

'Lost for words, darling?'

'Speechless.'

A tinkle of brittle laughter sounded down the line. 'If you had taken me seriously, it wouldn't have been necessary to go this far.'

Gabbi tightened her grip on the receiver. 'Don't be surprised if Tony hits you up for danger money. He received a knee in the groin and a few deep scratches.'

'The photographs are worth it. Show a little wis-

dom and start packing,' Annaliese suggested with sac-
charine sweetness.

'Benedict—'

'Will be shocked at the evidence.'

'Yes.'

There was a momentary silence.

'You can present me with the photos and the file
personally, Annaliese,' Benedict directed in a voice
so silk-smooth it sent shivers scudding down the
length of Gabbi's spine. 'If you're wise, you'll be
waiting at your front door with them in your hand ten
minutes from now. After which you'll explain to
Monique and James that you've received an urgent
call from your agent demanding your presence else-
where. So urgent,' he continued with deadly softness,
'that you need to board a plane tomorrow. I'll arrange
the airline ticket.

'If you should be sufficiently foolish to set foot in
Sydney again I'll lay charges against you for assault
and extortion. And don't,' he advised icily, 'put a
warning call through to the infamous Tony. There
isn't a place he can go that I won't eventually find
him. Do we understand each other?'

Benedict replaced the receiver with such care,
Gabbi felt afraid. With numbed fingers she replaced
the bathroom receiver onto the wall handset.

Her eyes were impossibly large as he crossed the
room, and she was powerless to utter so much as a
word when he lowered his head down to hers and took
reverent possession of her mouth.

'I'll be back.'

Then he was gone, with a swiftness that made her

shiver. Within minutes she heard an engine start up, and the refined purr as the car headed towards the gates. Then silence.

Gabbi discarded the towel and selected a pair of ivory satin pyjamas. She crossed to the large bed and turned back the covering. Then she sank down onto the stool in front of the mirrored dressing table and picked up her hairbrush.

It was twenty-five minutes later when Benedict re-entered the bedroom, and her arm slowed to a faltering halt as he moved to her side.

Her mouth trembled when he removed the brush from her hand.

'Where are they?' Was that her voice? It sounded so hushed it was almost indistinct.

'I destroyed them,' Benedict said gently.

She had to ask. 'Did you look at them?'

His hands curved over her shoulders. 'Yes.'

Her eyes filled, and she barely kept the tears at bay. 'I imagine they were—'

'Damning.'

A muscle contracted in one cheek. 'Would you have believed—?'

'No.' He touched a finger to her cheek, then trailed its tip to the corner of her mouth. 'They were intended to be held against you as blackmail.' He traced the fullness of her lower lip. 'What was the price, Gabbi?'

'Me,' she enlightened him with stark honesty. 'Out of your life.'

His hand slid to her throat and caressed the soft hollows at its base.

'You imagined I would let you go?'

'Annaliese was counting on it.'

His fingers slid to the top button of her pyjama shirt and dealt with it, before slipping down to the next one. The second button slid free, as did the third and last. Gently, he pulled the satin shirt free from her arms.

Gabbi watched his eyes darken as they rested on the pink smudges marking each pale globe.

'It's to be hoped the infamous Tony was well paid. Expert medical care can be expensive.'

Her mouth opened, then closed again as he brushed it with his own.

She shivered at the extent of his power. At how quickly he could exert it, and how far it could reach.

'You came home early,' Gabbi whispered. 'Why?'

His lips curved. 'Because I didn't want to spend another night away from you.'

Unbidden, the tears welled up and spilled, trickling down each cheek in twin rivulets. Gentle fingers tilted her chin, and she felt the touch of his mouth as it trailed one cheek, then the other, before he kissed each eyelid in turn.

'Don't,' Benedict bade her quietly.

She wanted to say she loved him. The words hovered near the edge of her lips, but remained unspoken.

'Tomorrow morning we're flying out to Hawaii.'

A protest rose to her lips. 'The office—'

'Can get by without us,' Benedict assured her as he scooped her into his arms.

'The Gibson deal—'

'James will handle it.'

'Benedict—'

'Shut up,' he ordered softly as he sank down onto the bed with her cradled on his lap.

Her pulse leapt then accelerated to a faster beat as his mouth brushed her temple then slid to the sensitive hollow beneath her ear.

She felt secure. And protected. For now, it was enough.

Gabbi's fingers worked the knot on his tie, then slid to the buttons on his shirt. 'I need to feel your skin next to mine.'

Benedict placed her carefully against the nest of pillows, then straightened to his feet. He didn't hurry, and she watched every movement as he divested himself of one garment after the other.

Then he came down onto the bed and pulled her to lie beside him. He propped himself up on an elbow and examined the soft mouth, the blue eyes looking at him with unblinking solemnity.

'Do you want to talk?'

Gabbi considered the question, then slowly shook her head. Tomorrow, maybe. Tonight she wanted the reassurance of his arms around her, his body intimately joined to hers.

Lifting a hand, she trailed his cheek with tentative fingers, and her eyes widened fractionally as he caught and carried them to his lips.

With infinite care he kissed them, one by one, before traversing to the bones at her wrist. Then he released her hand and bent his head to her breast, caressing each bruise with his mouth.

'Benedict.'

He lifted his head and met her gaze in silent query.

'I *need* you,' she said quietly, and saw desire flare in the dark eyes close to her own.

Her hands lifted to encircle his neck, and her mouth trembled beneath the soft touch of his before the pressure increased.

His tongue was an invasive entity as it explored the soft tissues, and she felt him tense as he found the abrasions where Tony had briefly ground his mouth against her own, heard the low growl of his anger, and sought to soothe it.

The slow reverence of his lovemaking made her want to cry, and afterwards she slept in his arms, her head pillowed against his chest.

CHAPTER ELEVEN

WAIKIKI BEACH was a glorious sight. Deep blue ocean, white sand, with multi-level high-rise hotels and apartment buildings lining the foreshore.

There were beaches to equal and surpass it in Australia, and many believed Queensland's Gold Coast to be comparable to Honolulu.

The climate was similar, the designer boutiques many and varied, but it was the cosmopolitan population and the friendly Hawaiian people which fascinated Gabbi.

It wasn't her first visit nor, she hoped, would it be her last.

Benedict had chosen the Royal Hawaiian hotel, known as the 'pink palace' due to its pink-washed exterior. Originally home to Hawaiian royalty, it held an aura of tradition and timelessness, and was unique in comparison to the many modern hotels bordering the foreshore. Crystal chandeliers featured in the foyer, and there was an abundance of luxurious Oriental rose-pink carpets.

Gracious was a word that sprang to mind, Gabbi decided as she sank into a chair and ordered a virgin piña colada from the hovering drinks waiter.

Five days of blissful relaxation had done wonders to repair her peace of mind, she mused as she gazed idly out to sea. Careful sunbathing had coloured her skin to a warm honey-gold.

By tacit agreement, they'd avoided the tourist attractions, choosing instead to commission a limousine with driver for a day to drive round the main island.

Shopping wasn't a priority, although she had explored some of the boutiques and made a few purchases.

'Feel like sharing?'

Gabbi pushed her sunglasses up on top of her head as she turned towards Benedict.

'My piña colada?' she countered with a teasing smile.

'You've been deep in thought for the past five minutes,' he drawled.

Gabbi allowed her gaze to wander towards a young woman whose slender, model-proportioned curves were unadorned except for a black thong-bikini brief. Tall, gorgeous and tanned, she seemed intent on spending equal time anointing her firm body with oil and worshipping the sun.

'I was just surveying the scene,' she said easily. 'And wondering where you're taking me to dinner.'

'Hungry?'

For you. Only you. Was it such a sin to want to be with one man so badly? To laugh, pleasure, *love him* so much that he became the very air that she breathed?

'Yes.' She wrinkled her nose at him. 'I think it must be all the fresh sea air and sunshine.'

A smile lifted the edges of his mouth. 'You get to choose.'

'Somewhere exotic, I think.'

'Define ''exotic''.'

'Soft lights, dreamy music, exquisitely presented food and—' she paused, her eyes filling with wicked warmth '—black-suited waiters who look as if they're just waiting to be discovered by some international film-studio executive.'

His eyelids drooped fractionally, and his expression was deceptively indolent. 'You have a particular restaurant in mind?'

A soft bubble of laughter emerged from her throat. 'Yes. It will be interesting to discover if one particular waiter still works there. He displayed such flair, such panache.' Her eyes gleamed with irrepressible humour. 'Definitely *sigh* material.'

'And did he sigh over you?'

'No more than that attractive, scantily clad brunette is sighing at the sight of you.' She hadn't missed the veiled interest or the subtle preening as the slim-curved beauty displayed her perfect body.

Benedict's gaze skimmed to the girl in question, assessed and dismissed her, and returned to Gabbi.

'Pleasant to look at.'

'Is that all you have to say?'

His eyes were dark, slumberous. 'She's not *you*.'

A flippant response rose to her lips, and died before it could be voiced. 'Words are easy,' she managed after a long silence.

'There's an axiom about actions speaking louder than words,' he offered, and she held his gaze, suddenly brave.

'Maybe I need both.'

He leaned forward in his chair and surveyed her expressive features. 'A verbal attestation of love?'

Gabbi tried for nonchalance and failed. 'Only if you mean it.' She tore her eyes away from his and looked beyond the pink and white striped canopies fronting the terrace to the distant horizon.

It seemed as if she'd waited ages for this precise moment. But now that it had come she wasn't sure she was ready. The breath seemed locked in her throat, suspending her breathing, and she was oblivious to the people around them, the dull chatter of voices, the soft background music.

'Look at me.'

It was a softly voiced command she chose not to ignore.

His features appeared sculpted, the gleam of artificial and fading natural light accentuating the strong planes and angles, toning his skin a deeper shade and highlighting the darkness of his hair.

For one brief second she was reminded of boardroom meetings where a glance from those deep dark eyes could lance a colleague's façade and reduce him to a quivering, inarticulate fool.

'*Love*, Gabbi?' A slow, warm smile lightened his features, and she caught a glimpse of the passion, the desire. And the need. 'I don't want to spend a day, a night without you by my side. You're sunshine and laughter.' He took hold of her hand and brought her palm to his lips and bestowed an evocative, open-mouthed kiss on its centre. 'Warmth and love. Everything.'

Heat coursed through her veins, sensitising nerve

cells until her whole body was an aching entity demanding his touch.

The words that had lain imprisoned in her heart for so long seemed hesitant to emerge. She swallowed, and saw that his eyes followed the movement.

A faint smile tugged at the corners of his mouth. 'Is it so difficult to reciprocate?' he queried gently.

Gabbi looked at him carefully. She hadn't expected to find vulnerability in any form. Yet it was there, in his eyes. A waiting, watchful quality that allowed her a glimpse of his inner soul.

There was a sense of wonder in the knowledge that she was probably the only one who would ever be permitted to witness it.

'The first day you entered the boardroom,' she began quietly, 'it was the embodiment of every cliché.' An impish smile curved her mouth. '*Electric*. I don't remember a word I said. Yet your words stayed engraved in my mind. Every gesture, every smile.' She reached up and touched the palm of her hand to his jaw. 'When James invited you to dinner, I think I knew, even then, the idea formulating in his mind. It should have mattered. But it didn't,' she said simply.

Benedict watched the play of emotions in her expressive eyes. They held few secrets from him. Soon they would hold none.

'I fell in love with *you*. Not Conrad Nicols' son and heir. If I hadn't felt like that, I would never have agreed to marriage.'

'Yet you chose to establish a façade,' he pursued, and her eyes remained steady.

'Monique congratulated me after the wedding.' The

words were almost painful as she forced them past the lump in her throat. 'On winning an eminently successful husband. I hadn't realised marrying you was a competition, or that Annaliese had been a contender.'

The leap of anger was clearly evident in the depths of his eyes. 'You believed her?'

'It all seemed to fit.' Too well, Gabbi reflected. 'Monique is James's wife. I would never say or do anything to destroy his happiness.'

'I don't share your generosity.'

'I can afford to be generous,' she said gently. And it was true.

The light was fading to dusk. Already the candles were being lit outside on the terrace tables, and electric lamps provided a welcome glow.

A faint smile tilted the edges of Gabbi's mouth. 'Are you going to feed me?'

His features softened. 'We could always order Room Service.'

The smile deepened. 'The food is superb at the Sheraton Waikiki's restaurant.' Set on a high floor, the restaurant offered panoramic views from every window. She cast him a teasing glance. 'We could dance a little, linger over coffee.'

'If that's what you want.'

She laughed, a light, bubbly sound that echoed her happiness and deepened the teasing gleam in her eyes. 'It'll suffice, for a few hours.'

'And afterwards?'

'We have the night.'

A low chuckle escaped from his throat. 'Sounds interesting.'

Gabbi fought the temptation to lean forward and kiss him. 'You can count on it.'

She made no protest as he stood and pulled her to her feet. Then together they walked down to the main entrance and crossed the path to the Sheraton Waikiki hotel.

It was early, and there was a choice of several empty tables. Gabbi chose one by the window, and Benedict ordered champagne—Cristal.

The food was presented with imaginative flair, and each course was a superb attestation to the chef's culinary skill.

'Magical,' Gabbi declared as she glanced at the fairy tracery of lit high-rise buildings lining the darkening foreshore as it curved towards Diamond Head.

'Yes.'

Except Benedict wasn't looking at the view. A delicate blush coloured her cheeks at the degree of warmth evident as his gaze lingered on her features.

'Shall we dance?'

When they reached the dance floor he gathered her close, and she melted against him, unselfconsciously lifting her arms to link her hands together at his nape.

The music was slow and dreamy, the lights low, and she rested against him as they drifted together. Her body stirred, warming with the promise of passion.

It was quite remarkable, she mused, how she could almost feel the blood coursing through her veins, the heavy, faster beat of her heart. And the kindling fire deep within her that slowly invaded every nerve, every cell, until she was aware of nothing else but a deep, physical need for more than his touch.

Yet there was a certain pleasure in delaying the moment when they would leave and wander back to their suite. It heightened the senses, deepened the desire, and slowly drove her wild.

His breath whispered against her ear. 'Let's get out of here.'

She lifted her face and brushed his lips with her own. 'Soon.'

As soon as they reached their table a waiter appeared.

'Would you care for coffee? A liqueur?'

Benedict deferred the decision to Gabbi, and his eyes assumed a musing gleam when she agreed with the waiter that a liqueur coffee would be an excellent choice with which to end the meal.

It was late when they entered their suite, and Gabbi slid off her heeled sandals, then reached to loosen the pins confining her hair.

His hands closed over her shoulders and pulled her close, then he lowered his head and took possession of her mouth.

Heat suffused her body, bringing it achingly alive. A tiny groan emerged from her throat as his lips slid down the sensitive cord of her neck, teased the hollows, then trailed the edge of her gown.

Layer by layer they slowly dispensed with their clothes, and Gabbi stifled a moan as Benedict began a slow tasting of each breast before tracing a path down to savour the most intimate crevice of all.

She felt the initial wave of sensation and gloried in it, and caught the next, exulting in each successive contraction as she rode higher and higher before soaring over the precipice to sensual nirvana.

It was so intensely erotic that her whole body shook with emotional involvement, and afterwards she lay still, enjoying the gentle drift of his fingers over her skin.

With one sinuous movement she rose up and placed her lips against his, initiating a long, evocative kiss. Now it was his turn, and she took her time, treasuring each indrawn breath, every tensed muscle, the faint sound deep in his throat as she teased and tantalised.

So much power, harnessed, yet almost totally beneath her control. It was a heady sensation to take him to the brink, and see how long she could hold him there before he tumbled her down beside him.

His possession was swift, and she gasped at the level of his penetration, arching again and again as she rose to meet each deep thrust.

Afterwards he rolled onto his back, carrying her with him, and he cradled her close, his lips brushing across her temple as he trailed his fingers lazily up and down her spine.

'I love you.' She felt fulfilled and at peace. Gone were the agonising afterthoughts, the wishful longing for something more.

Benedict slid a hand beneath her chin and sought her mouth with his own in a slow, sweet kiss.

Afterwards she settled her head down onto his chest.

'Comfortable?'

'Mmm,' she murmured sleepily. 'Want me to move?'

Gentle fingers stroked through her hair. 'No.'

Gabbi smiled and pressed her lips into the hollow at the base of his throat. This was as close to heaven as it was possible to get.

'How do you feel about babies?'

'In general?'

'Ours.'

The fingers stilled. 'Are you trying to tell me something?'

Her lips teased a path along his collarbone. 'It should be a mutual decision, don't you think?'

'Gabbi.' Her name emerged as a soft growl, and she smiled.

'Is that a yes, or a no?'

'Of course—*yes*. The thought of you enceinte is enough to—'

A husky laugh escaped from her throat. 'Mmm,' she murmured appreciatively as she felt his length harden and extend deep within her. 'Such a positive reaction.'

Benedict's possession of her mouth was an evocative experience, and she sighed as she trailed a butterfly caress along the edge of his jaw.

'I'd like to continue my role with Stanton-Nicols. Flexibility, an office at home when I'm pregnant and afterwards...' She deliberated, her expressive eyes becoming pensive. 'Once the children are in school I'd like to return to the city. Part-time,' she added, knowing she'd want to be home to greet them, to be involved in their extra-curricular activities.

She indulged herself in a fleeting image of a small, dark-haired boy, a petite, pale-haired girl. Ball practice, swimming lessons, ballet, music, gymnastics. Homework. Walks in the park, picnics at the beach. Laughter. *Family*. And Benedict. Dear God, always Benedict at her side.

'I love you,' Gabbi reiterated quietly.

Benedict kissed her deeply, then slowly rolled until she lay beneath him. 'You're my life,' he assured her simply, and kissed her again.

She gave a satisfied sigh as he began to move, and she linked her hands together behind his neck.

Magic, she concluded a long time later as she lay curved close against his side. Sheer magic. The merging of two bodies, two souls, in a mutual exploration of pleasure. And love. *Always* love.

Take 4 bestselling love stories FREE

Plus get a FREE surprise gift!

Special Limited-time Offer

Mail to Harlequin Reader Service®

3010 Walden Avenue
P.O. Box 1867
Buffalo, N.Y. 14240-1867

YES! Please send me 4 free Harlequin Presents® novels and my free surprise gift. Then send me 6 brand-new novels every month, which I will receive months before they appear in bookstores. Bill me at the low price of $2.90 each plus 25¢ delivery and applicable sales tax, if any*. That's the complete price and a savings of over 10% off the cover prices—quite a bargain! I understand that accepting the books and gift places me under no obligation ever to buy any books. I can always return a shipment and cancel at any time. Even if I never buy another book from Harlequin, the 4 free books and the surprise gift are mine to keep forever.

106 BPA A3UL

Name _____ (PLEASE PRINT)

Address _____ Apt. No. _____

City _____ State _____ Zip _____

This offer is limited to one order per household and not valid to present Harlequin Presents® subscribers. *Terms and prices are subject to change without notice. Sales tax applicable in N.Y.

UPRES-698   ©1990 Harlequin Enterprises Limited

HARLEQUIN ◆ PRESENTS®

Coming in September...

Breaking Making Up

by
**Miranda Lee and
Susan Napier**

Two original stories in one unique volume—
"Two for the price of one!"

Meet two irresistible men from
Down Under— one Aussie, one Kiwi.
The time has come for them to settle old scores
and win the women they've always wanted!

Look for *Breaking Making Up* (#1907)
in September 1997.

Available wherever Harlequin books are sold.

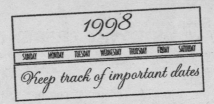

Three beautiful and colorful calendars that celebrate some of the most popular trends in America today.

Look for:

Just Babies—a 16 month calendar that features a full year of absolutely adorable babies!

1998 CALENDAR
Just Babies
16 months of adorable bundles of joy!

Hometown Quilts
1998 Calendar
A 16 month quilting extravaganza!

Hometown Quilts—a 16 month calendar featuring quilted art squares, plus a short history on twelve different quilt patterns.

Inspirations—a 16 month calendar with inspiring pictures and quotations.

Inspirations

A 16 month calendar that will lift your spirits and gladden your heart

Steeple Hill™

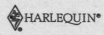

HARLEQUIN®

Value priced at $9.99 U.S./$11.99 CAN., these calendars make a perfect gift!

Available in retail outlets in August 1997.　　CAL98

Free Gift Offer

With a Free Gift proof-of-purchase
from any Harlequin® book, you can receive
a beautiful cubic zirconia pendant.

This stunning marquise-shaped stone is a genuine cubic
zirconia—accented by an 18" gold tone necklace.
(Approximate retail value $19.95)

Send for yours today...
compliments of HARLEQUIN®

To receive your free gift, a cubic zirconia pendant, send us one original proof-of-
purchase, photocopies not accepted, from the back of any Harlequin Romance®,
Harlequin Presents®, Harlequin Temptation®, Harlequin Superromance®, Harlequin
Intrigue®, Harlequin American Romance®, or Harlequin Historicals® title available at
your favorite retail outlet, together with the Free Gift Certificate, plus a check or money
order for $1.65 U.S./$2.15 CAN. (do not send cash) to cover postage and handling,
payable to Harlequin Free Gift Offer. We will send you the specified gift. Allow 6 to 8
weeks for delivery. Offer good until December 31, 1997, or while quantities last. Offer
valid in the U.S. and Canada only.

Free Gift Certificate

Name: _____

Address: _____

City: _____ State/Province: _____ Zip/Postal Code: _____

Mail this certificate, one proof-of-purchase and a check or money order for postage
and handling to: HARLEQUIN FREE GIFT OFFER 1997. In the U.S.: 3010 Walden
Avenue, P.O. Box 9071, Buffalo NY 14269-9057. In Canada: P.O. Box 604, Fort Erie,
Ontario L2Z 5X3.

FREE GIFT OFFER   084-KEZ

ONE PROOF-OF-PURCHASE

To collect your fabulous FREE GIFT, a cubic zirconia pendant, you must include this
original proof-of-purchase for each gift with the properly completed Free Gift Certificate.

084-KEZR